DEATH
by Pallet Knife

A Saugatuck Murder Mystery

by

G Corwin Stoppel

Lord Hiltensweiller Press

Published by Lord Hiltensweiller Press, Saugatuck, Michigan, 49453
lordhilt@gmail.com

Cover design by S. Winthers

ISBN-13: 978-1548072810

ISBN-10: 1548072818

Joyfully dedicated
to my
Grand-nephew
Tygh Madsen

INTRODUCTION

I have always and most scrupulously adhered to my grandfather's admonition that the only way of being certain of arriving on time is to be ten minutes early. The exception is when I am flying. My days of making a mad dash through a crowded airport terminal to arrive at the boarding gate with seconds to spare is at least three and a half decades in the past. Now, I arrive early to make my way through check-in and security, then meander up to the lounge with plenty of time to find a seat. Preferably, it is a seat near the window because planes have fascinated me since I was a youngster.

On one particularly important day a summer or two ago, I had no more than made myself marginally comfortable when the announcement board went from green to yellow, indicating a delay. The memory of my grandfather growling under his breath, getting louder by the second, until he roared, "Thunderation! I'm in the waiting room again!" came to mind. I hadn't thought about his impatience for years, and it made me smile. It terrified me when I was young; not being one of life's happier memories. I was indeed in the proverbial waiting room.

I usually avoid the little airport shops, all of them crammed with over-priced merchandise I neither need nor want. Once you have seen one, you have seen them all. But, that day, with time to spare, I wandered down the hall to a glorified cubbyhole packed with junk food, candy, and trinkets. I by-passed them, heading for the magazine racks and book shelves in the back, hoping to find something, anything, of interest. The full-price best sellers are always at eye level, lower ranking books on the shelves that go from chest to knee, and at the bottom are the books whose next stop would be the deep discount bin at the front of the big box bookstores. After that, they end up in recycling. Down near my ankles was something that caught my eye: the word, "Saugatuck."

I happen to know there are only two cities in the nation with that name. One is in Connecticut; the other is my hometown in Michigan. I had a fifty-fifty chance it would be the right town, the one in Michigan, so I picked it up. The cover was certainly appealing: An alluring woman, the silhouette of a fedora-topped man, and the Big Pavilion. I'd hit the jackpot and bought the book. It was only when I started reading the first chapter of *The Great Saugatuck Murder Mystery* that I felt the cold shiver of a ghost hovering around my shoulders. This wasn't just a tale about my hometown. It was my story! The tale of a retired surgeon and his brother, my mother and me: Phoebe Walters.

As luck would have it, I was on my way to Grand Rapids, just forty miles north-east of Saugatuck, to attend a convention. It didn't take long to decide to attend the convention's opening reception and cocktail party that evening, work the room for a while to see people and be seen, and then take a powder the next morning to go down to Saugatuck and have a look around. After all, when a ghost out of the past drops in for a visit, you might as well take time to shake hands.

Right after breakfast the next morning I sweet-talked a condescending young woman at a car rental desk into entrusting me with a set of keys. For some reason she felt it was necessary to talk very loudly and very slowly as we went through the paper work. She was very anxious that I could find my way without getting lost. "Oh, it's simple," I told her. "Grand Rapids, south to Hudsonville, past Zeeland and Holland, and then get off the highway and onto the state road. They're all paved, you know." She didn't seem impressed with that comment, ignored my sarcasm and asked I needed a map. A map? Who uses a map anymore? But maybe she didn't think I was sufficiently tech-savvy to understand a GPS device. She was even less impressed when I suggested an upgrade to a Corvette or Mustang with a turbo-charged Hemi engine. She asked if maybe I would like something else. I flashed a smile at her. "I don't suppose you have a Dodge Super Bee, do you? Preferably neon orange. Now, that was a car. Punch it and you can feel your stomach bounce off your backbone. My mother loved hers."

Instead, she foisted an underpowered dull little brown Chrysler 200 on me. I swear it was powered by a trio of geriatric gerbils. Automatic transmission, too. That was no fun. I wanted to burn a little rubber pulling out of the lot.

I cruised slowly up and down Butler and Water Streets, resisting the urge to blow my horn at some fellow driving a little green car, and looking at everything and everyone. I realized Saugatuck hadn't changed all that much since when I was growing up, other than a lot of it was different. Our old house, and the Wilson place next to it were gone, replaced by a mansion. The coal shed where we took on fuel for grandfather's boat was gone. Koening's Hardware two story brick building was still there, but it had change hands. I wondered if the old potbellied stove was still there and if some of the old boys still sat around it to tell stories. Across the street was the Maplewood Hotel, still the same as it always had been, except the paint job was better. Bobbie and her switchboard were a thing of the past, of course. As I trailed slowly behind the elderly Barney Oldfield, I saw the other buildings I recognized. There was a parking spot in front of the old Post Office which was now an art gallery, and from the sign, owned by a fellow named Brandess. Jim Brandess. I'd read about him in letters Sylvia and Jane, two of mother's friends, had sent me. Some of his paintings were in the front window, and I could tell the artist knew which end of the brush to use.

One thing that hadn't changed was jay-walking. I cut across the street to stop by Parrish's Drugstore and maybe get a bit of information. The building was the same; the sign indicated it had new owners. And, they'd kept the soda fountain. That brought back wonderful memories.

"Let me get that for you," an older fellow said, stepping in front of me to pull open the door. I thanked him and paused."You look familiar," I told him. "Henry Gleason, am I right? You are Henry, aren't you?" He looked puzzled that I would know him, then laughed when I told him who I was, reminding him that we hadn't seen each other since Mother's funeral years ago.

"It's been a long time. I still think about her from time to time. Say, I guess you know everyone's been reading about you and your family."

"So I've heard," I said. "That's what brought me back here for a quick visit. I don't suppose there are many of our generation still around."

"No. No, I guess not. Sylvia died a few years back. Now, you'd remember Peggy Boyce; she still lives here in town. Say, you know what? They made her the Citizen of the Year this spring, and about time, too! And, maybe you didn't hear, but Jane van Dis passed a few months ago. She gave up being Lady Liberty in the Fourth of July parades a while back. RJ's still alive and kicking!" he told me.

"Still kicking and whistling" I corrected him. That made him laugh. Henry assured me that yes, he was still whistling.

I offered to buy him a cup of coffee, but he said he had to get back to the Star of Saugatuck ticket office and get ready for the day, explaining that his daughter-in-law kept him busy. He added that the soda fountain wouldn't be open for a while, but I could get a cup across the street at Pumpernickel's Restaurant, or half a block farther down at the Sand Bar.

The Sand Bar? That caught my attention. According to the mystery book, that's where the story, where MY story, started. "You know where it is. Used to be Domenic's Barber Shop, remember that place. Bet you never went in there, did you? You could get shaved in the chair or at the table by a hustler," he chuckled. He was right. Mother would never let me go into a barbershop and pool hall.

The writer had it pegged right. It really was an old-fashioned small town bar – long, narrow, and dark, the air still heavy with stale beer. I looked it over. A bar to the left side, some tables and chairs opposite it. A television was on, with the volume turned down. A pair of older men, probably morning regulars, were perched on stools reading the *Commercial Record* newspapers. They ignored me until I asked if one of them was Billy.

"That's me," one of them answered. "We don't open until ten, but if you'd like some coffee..."

I liked that idea. "That's what I came for," I said as I perched on a stool next to them, and drank some harsh black coffee. Billy introduced me to his companion. "This is Tommy. You just passing through or visiting for a few days?"

"Just a short visit. I'd read a mystery about Saugatuck, and I was hoping to look around. Maybe I might get to meet the author. By any chance do you know him or where I could find him?"

Thomas, as I soon learned he preferred to be called, burst out laughing. "Everyone in town knows him. I used to be his secretary. He drops in for coffee once in a while." I watched as he reached for an old-fashioned flip-phone and punched in the numbers. "Cory,

Thomas. Am I interrupting you? Good. Where are you right now? The bank? Good. Say, can you come over to the Sand Bar? There's a young lady here who wants to meet you. No, go ahead and finish up, and come over."

A few minutes later he walked in the door. "Padre, better hold onto something tight," Thomas told him, "and meet Phoebe Walters."

He stared at me, took a pipe out of his mouth, and looked like he wanted to say something, but couldn't find the words. "First time I've ever known Father Cory to be speechless!" Billy laughed.

I reached out to shake hands with him. "Phoebe. Phoebe Walters. The girl from the story you wrote, remember?"

"Really?" he asked.

"Really!"

For the next hour or so, all of us talked, and I told the three men a few more stories about my grandfather. And they had a few stories to tell me about my mother in her later years; stories I hadn't heard before. I asked if she ever came into the Sand Bar. "No, but she and Gracie Wilson used to go down to the Butler every morning for a glass of milk with a shot of whiskey in it." Thomas wrinkled up his nose at the thought of their tipple.

We brought up the names of a lot of other old-timers, mostly gone now, and then Billy asked, "So, what I want to know is if you and your grandfather ever had any other adventures?

I smiled and pointed to a painting behind the bar off to the left side near a sign advertising pickled eggs. It was just plain ugly. One of those over-wrought high-Renaissance Italian pieces of a well rounded young woman wearing just a whisk of strategically placed fabric around her waist, leaning on a red couch and eating a handful of grapes. "First, you must tell me where that painting came from," I said.

"Oh there was a fellow around here named Gordon, 'Part-Time' we called him because he wasn't what you would call a steady work-er. He was always finding stuff he thought was too good to throw away," Billy said. "He pawned it and said he'd pay me back, but that was an old story with him. Anyway, after he died I left it up there, sort of a tribute to him. Why? Don't tell me it's worth something!"

I pushed my empty cup towards the fellow on the other side of the bar, nodding that I would like a refill. "Well, let me tell you about it," I said.

"When was it?" Thomas asked.

"It was the next summer, when Grandfather came back again...." I said, watching as Father Stoppel pulled out a notebook and pen.

CHAPTER ONE

Doctor Horace Balfour, Phoebe's grandfather, had planned to return to Saugatuck in time for the Fourth of July parade and fireworks, but a 'medical situation' as he casually called it, had delayed him for several weeks while he was laid up at a hospital in Chicago. Just what had happened, he wasn't saying, even to his brother Theo and his wife Clarice, who had hurried by train from northern Minnesota to see him. "It was a bit of silly stupidity, that's all!" he told them, and made it clear that when they got to Saugatuck he didn't want to worry Phoebe. Theo, who could usually draw out information from a doctor or nurse without having to 'pull rank' wasn't getting anywhere with the hospital staff. "They're more afraid of him than anything else," he fussed to Clarice.

"Well, that's true to form," she sighed. "And him not telling you much, either."

Suffice it to note, once he was out of danger, Horace was not a stellar patient. Being laid up in a hospital bed was not easy for him. It was far worse for the doctors and especially for the nurses, who were doing their best to care for him. He bellowed and complained, constantly suggesting different types of care and procedures, even supervising how his dressings were changed. When a new nurse reminded him that he was her patient and not a doctor, his eyes widened in fury. She stared him down, telling him, "Oh, go throw that bedpan if you like. It will remind me of when I was on a pediatric unit where not all of the patients were so badly behaved. Some of them already knew how to say 'please and thank you, nurse.'" He settled down after that, but the whole staff breathed a sigh of relief when he was discharged.

"It's a pity we already have our summer clothes on the boat," Theo fussed to his wife. "I'd just as soon go home and let him luxuriate in his own misery."

"Now, be nice. He IS your brother, after all," she cautioned him. "You know very well he'd look after you."

Theo growled in futile frustration.

To his credit, he settled down once he was on his boat, the *Aurora*, and Captain Garwood had cast off from the Chicago Pier and set the course for Saugatuck. Even so, he still refused to listen to anyone's idea of how he should convalesce. When Clarice suggested he might be more comfortable lounging in his pyjamas, robe, and carpet slippers, he growled that he was a gentleman and would be properly dressed for the summer: shoes, socks, shirt and tie, and his white linen suit. It was that, he told them or otherwise he would stay in his cabin. Every morning he gritted his teeth through the pain of dressing and going up to his library to collapse in his leather chair and read. Trailing close behind was Mrs. Garwood or Clarice, holding his cane and reminding him to use it, keeping a close eye on him so he wouldn't tumble.

"It is a walking stick! Canes are for old women!" he barked at them. Even Clarice had better sense than to tell him that canes were for old women AND old men. He growled a protracted "Thunderation!" beneath his breath.

Every morning when Mrs. Garwood brought him his glass of orange juice, he would remind her that when they got to Saugatuck he wanted whitefish for his first dinner. One morning she glared at him, "You won't even get to Saugatuck to see your granddaughter if you don't behave yourself!" She stalked off to emphasize her point, and for the next few hours he settled down.

On Doctor Theo's orders, Captain Gar had kept the ship at three quarters speed, slowing to half or quarter speed when his brother was resting. It stretched out the trip from Chicago along the coast of Lake Michigan, giving what they hoped would be more time to recuperate. "Just remember, we're doing this for Phoebe, not him," Theo had said. "He's only being cantankerous because something is eating at him. He'll be nicer once he's feeling better. Gar doubted Horace would tolerate their slow progress, and when Horace did complain, Gar somehow managed to convince him they were going as fast as the old paddle wheeler could go against the water. Horace just growled.

Over lunch the next day Horace again questioned the captain. "Are we malingering at this speed to skimp on coal? No problems with the boilers or pipes are there? The pistons are all working well, are they?" The captain assured him all was well with the *Aurora*. "Thunderation, man! Get the speed up! The idea is to get to Saugatuck this year, before the ice settles in! This year, not just in the nick of time for the girl's high school graduation! Full speed ahead!"

Gar took it all in stride. "Glad to know you're feeling some better, Doctor. You get us all worried up when you're not fussing and fuming about something, and go all quiet on us. We're just not used to you that way. Scares me. Scares the missus, too. Now, everything is just fine with the boat, but you're not taking into account snags in the water, and how some of the sand bars have shifted. We don't want to ram a log or get hung up, you know. That would really put a crimp in our plans."

Horace paused to think it over. "Well, that makes sense. Now, if we went farther out we could avoid the sand bars. Take her out into deeper water and get the speed up."

"No, Sir! Not with a flat bottomed antique like this. Not if the wind comes up at any time. It would be different if we were on a lake or a river, but not this big lake. Better safe than sorry. We'll be there in another day, two at the most."

The next evening, an hour before twilight, they tied up at the pier in South Haven. "We could keep on going and still get there tonight if you'd just pour on the coal!" Doctor Horace muttered. No one listened to him. "Well, at least send a radio message to Phoebe that we'll be home tomorrow morning," he told Gar.

The captain smiled. "It's already been done. And, I told the girl we'd fire the cannon once we cleared the breakwater to come up-river."

The old doctor smiled, then took off his straw boater and used his pocket square to wipe off the sweatband. He put it back on at an angle. Mrs. Garwood, who saw him from the doorway of the galley, was smiling. It meant he was already in a better mood.

Horace and Theo were having their morning coffee on deck when Clarice joined them, pointing out they were passing the Oval Beach. "Beautiful, isn't it?" Horace asked. Fred, Horace's driver, and increasingly his right hand man, joined them with the same news. "Well, you want the honour of letting Phoebe know we're coming upriver?" Horace asked.

"Yes, Sir! I sure do! Can't wait to see that girl and her mother again. I've missed them much as you. Well, maybe almost as much as you, Boss."

Horace allowed himself a rare chuckle. "Then put in a full charge. Let her know we're on our way!" Fred gave a big smile and hurried to fire the signal cannon.

They could feel Gar swing the wheel hard to port, taking the *Aurora* in a slow, wide arch out farther into the lake, lining up the bow between the two breakwaters. He checked the wind on the flag on the bow, then telegraphed Royce down in the engine room to full stop so he could get the feel of the current and find the plume of the Kalamazoo River. Satisfied, he signalled half-speed ahead, and swung the wheel to starboard, feeling the current push against them as he straightened out. Several long pulls on the whistle alerted the other boaters of his intention. "We're in the river!" he shouted through his megaphone to his passengers.

"Fire when ready, Fred!" Doctor Horace commanded. He and Theo watched him light the fuse, then dart well out of the way. "Only time I see Fred move that fast," Theo observed. Even without shot in the barrel, no one had any confidence that one day the old cannon wouldn't crack or blow apart. They waited, wondering if the fuse had burned out, then heard the cannon bark and belch out white smoke.

"You think I ought to do it once more, just to be sure Miss Phoebe heard it?" Fred hinted.

"Sure! Why not? Give them another one! Make it good and loud!" Horace said. The two of them were smiling with sheer pleasure.

"You know, Horace, for all your dignity and reserve, you're just boys at heart. The both of you! You two just cannot resist something that goes boom, can you?" Clarice teased, holding her husband's arm. The three of them watched Fred swab the barrel, reload, and fire a second blast.

Gar reduced the boat to half-speed as they passed the breakwater and got into the channel, making a slow stately entrance toward Saugatuck. As they approached the village, Doctor Horace called Mrs. Garwood from the galley to join him on deck. "Now, I would like you to look over to port. Do you see those three little buildings up ahead? And another one beyond them? Those are fishing shacks used by commercial fishermen. Keep their locations in mind, because I have it on good authority they can very easily be reached by road. Now, do you know what those men do? Every day they risk their lives to go out in their boats to catch fish. Not just any old fish, but whitefish. Whitefish, Mrs. Garwood! They bring them back to their shack so they can be sold. They sell them to customers just like you. They truly yearn for you to walk into their place, buy their fish, and bring them back home to cook to perfection. That's what they live for. Each and every night they crawl into their beds, deliriously happy that you bought and cooked their fish. All night long they dream sweet dreams of a nice, intelligent woman, you Mrs. Garwood, returning many times throughout the summer. Now, I know you don't want to disappoint them, do you? You don't want to dash and shatter their dreams, do you? So, do you get my drift so we understand each other, Mrs. Garwood?"

"Oh, are you saying you would like whitefish for dinner sometime, Doctor Balfour?" she teased.

"Thunderation, woman! Yes, that is precisely what I am saying!"

She looked at him thoughtfully, nodding her head up and down. "In that case, I will take your suggestion under advisement."

The *Aurora* elegantly steamed up river, the two red paddlewheels churning up the water, with Gar blowing the whistle to acknowledge and return greetings from the other boats. People on shore waved at them as they passed. "I'll never figure out why people like to wave at boats," Horace said absently.

"Maybe it's because they like to be friendly to strangers; like smiling. Some people truly enjoy smiling at other people. You ought to give it a try sometime, Horace," Theo told him. "It might not make sense to you, but people do like to do it. Give it a whirl and see what you think."

At the wide part of the river, what some locals called "the lake" and what some first-time visitors and day-trippers mistook for Lake Michigan, Gar made a slow pirouette, reduced the speed, and let the boat glide downstream with the current. Two young men in a canoe, trying to get a closer look, were rebuffed with a long blast of the whistle and a few muttered words from the captain. He signalled full stop, then reverse, and full stop again as he swung the wheel hard to starboard, then back to the center. With only the slightest bump, they were lined up against the dock.

"Well done, Captain Gar!" Theo shouted up to him. Gar answered with a tip of his cap and a bow, then began shouting orders to several young men who caught the ropes to secure the boat to the dock.

Doctor Horace ignored all of that. He was too busy scanning the sidewalks, watching for Phoebe to come running toward him, and was disappointed when she wasn't anywhere in sight. He didn't realize that she was right in front of him, and when he did, was surprised to see she had grown several inches over the past months.

For days, maybe for weeks, Phoebe had rehearsed in her mind exactly what she was going to do the moment she saw her grandfather. She reminded herself she was a young lady now, and young ladies are not supposed to show too much excitement or get carried away with giddiness. "Paris manners!" she had repeated her mother's constant admonition time and again, even as she heard the cannon boom the first time. She checked the blue bow in her hair in the mirror, straightened her dress, and forced herself to walk, not run, down Water Street. Along the way she reminded herself that she would wave, and wait for the gangplank to be lowered all the way down, count to five, and finally walk up to greet her grandfather.

The minute the gangplank was close enough to the ground, she jumped onto it and raced as fast as possible to wrap herself around her grandfather. "You're home again!" she said as she hugged him again. After Doctor Horace then Uncle Theo and Aunt Clarice.

"Phoebe, you've grown. You're taller!" Horace said in genuine astonishment.

"I believe, Doctor, that it is quite natural for children to do that," Theo said in mock seriousness. "It happens almost all the time. Nothing for you to worry about. I'm surprised you didn't pick that up in medical school."

Clarice leaned closer to her husband and whispered, "Seeing her again is the best medicine in the world for him. He's smiling. If this keeps up he might join the human race someday."

"Be nice," Theo told her. "Horace is just different than most people. But he was very relieved that Horace seemed to come alive once again.

"You want your lemonade neat or on the rocks?" Horace teased Phoebe.

"Why, neat, of course! Just the way you like your lemonade. Besides, you get more lemonade that way if you don't put ice in the glass!"

"Mrs. Garwood, it looks like lemonade all around – for everyone. Two of them straight up, please, one for me and one for my best girl!" Horace beamed. "Fred, you too, and someone get Royce up here. Captain, Mrs. Garwood, you've earned it and then some. Let's have our lemonade first, and then we'll get the car out on dry land. Later, young lady, we'll see about going for some Green Rivers. Shall we make it Crappel's or Parrish's?"

"Well, either one is jake with me. Or, we could do both! We could have our Green Rivers at Parrish's because they make the best, and then we can go over to Crappel's to get some store-bought ice cream for tonight! Sound good to you?" she asked.

He tipped his head back and laughed. "That's jake with me, too. Best not tell your mother we're having two desserts. She might not approve. Where is she, anyway? I was hoping she could be here by now."

Phoebe looked down the street toward the chain ferry. "She'll be coming as soon as she can. Mother said she had some extra work to do at Ox-Bow. Some things to figure out," she answered a bit too quietly. Clarice caught the hidden message and raised her eyebrows. Horace missed the finer nuance of her voice.

"Well, after we finish our lemonade we could ask Fred to drive us up there and give her a ride back," Horace suggested.

"We'd better not. She doesn't like being interrupted when she's got too much to do. Besides, I'm sure it won't be all that much longer. And, I'm sure she heard you shoot off the cannon. I'll bet everyone in town heard it! Maybe they thought it was a pirate ship!" She took a long sip of her drink, stalling for time, before quietly asking. "You wrote to me when you were in England. Did you bring anything home you want to show me?"

"You mean, did I bring you a present? Well, you know, there just might be something for you in my library. Come on, I'll show you." He pulled himself up and reached for his silver-headed walking stick, steadying himself against the table for a moment.

Phoebe gasped in horror. "Grandfather! Why are you using that cane? Are you sick or something?"

"Oh, it's nothing serious. Sometimes when people get just a little bit older they get a little unsteady on their feet." He held it up for her to see. "You don't want me to fall down, now do you? Besides, I think I look rather dashing when I carry it, don't you?" He didn't wait for her answer as he led her across the deck. They paused at the library door. "Remember these?" he asked.

"I sure do! That's from when you had a shoot out with the entire Capone gang last summer, and saved Saugatuck and everything. Everyone knows about it! Bobbie Smith even wanted my autograph just because you're my grandfather!"

"Hope you gave him one! Don't forget, you had a big part in it, climbing up to the wheel house to send messages to the Coast Guard to come and help us out of a jam. But, the entire Capone gang? All of them? Well, now that's a story that has grown since last summer – just like you. You know, you're going to be as tall as me if you keep this up!" Horace turned around toward his brother. "You hear that Theo? We stopped the whole Capone gang singlehanded. That's a good one!"

"Better not let Snarky get wind of that or he'll want to settle the score this year."

Horace sat down behind his desk and handed Phoebe her present, wrapped in brown paper and tied with string. "This is for you. I was at a medical conference and ran into my favorite author. Go on. Rip that paper off and tell me what you think."

At first, Phoebe didn't look very thrilled, even if it was a gift from her grandfather. She could tell it was a book, and she hoped it wasn't going to be a medical book or something she couldn't understand. Or, worse, a Bible. Grownups were always giving Bibles to her and her friends. She already had four of them. She opened it carefully, prepared for the worst. "It's *The Hound of the Baskervilles*," she said slowly as she read the cover. She opened the cover and found it inscribed, For Phoebe Walters, the granddaughter of my very good American friend, Horace Balfour, MD, from Arthur

Conan Doyle MD, with a little help from my colleague Dr. John Watson."

"Is Sherlock Holmes a doctor like you?" she asked, confused.

"Well, not quite. You know that his friend, John Watson, is a doctor, and so is Arthur Conan Doyle. We met up at a conference in London, and I thought of you. Now, you have an autographed copy of his book. Take good care of it because it is always going to remind you of our summers together in Saugatuck."

"We're going to have lots more summers!" she said fiercely.

"Lots more! I'm counting on that. Now, sit down and tell me everything happening in your life. Tell me something good, really, really good."

Phoebe let out a long sigh, and then for the next few minutes she told him about school and her friends, and how much she was enjoying the shortwave radio set he had given her at Christmas. "And, now that I have my license, I've gotten my code up to twenty-five words a minute. How about that! Mr. Jenkins down at the Western Union said he would hire me on the spot if I was older, even if I was a girl because there aren't many girls who are up to twenty-five anywhere in the whole country. I might even be the first!"

"Were older, Phoebe, not was. If you were older. Go on. So, what do you do with it?" he asked, not quite understanding how a radio telegraph worked, much less why a girl her age would be interested in it.

Phoebe let out another long sigh of exasperation. Telling grown-ups about things could be so hard. "Well, I come home from school and do my homework, and after Mother checks it, I go up to my room and turn it on. We radio operators call the radio room our 'shack'. And, then I listen to see if anyone is sending out a CQ.

That's our way of asking, 'seeking you' which means they want to talk to someone."

"I see. But you don't really talk, do you? You send dots and dashes back and forth. Then what happens?"

"Well, if someone is sending a CQ I might answer it. And, if there isn't anyone on that frequency, then I send out my CQ to see if anyone is listening. Sometimes, if the skip is right, I can talk to people all over the country, or even all the way to England."

"Okay. Slow down. The skip? What's that?" he asked.

"Oh, you would have to ask! I really don't understand it myself," Phoebe said slowly, "but it has something to do with the atmosphere. Sometimes, a signal comes from half-way around the world, and sometimes I can barely pick up Grand Rapids. It's always better late at night or in the winter."

"I see. And, when you do reach someone, what do you talk about?"

The girl brightened up again. "All sorts of things! Where we are and how strong their signal is coming in, and how strong my signal is. Sometimes I even get an S-10."

"Am I to take it an S-10 is good?"

"Oh, it's the absolute best. It's as strong a signal as you can get. I got an S-10 twice last week, and then when Captain Gar sent a message yesterday, it came in an S-10. That's really exciting. But the one last week was from Come-by-Chance in Newfoundland. That's a funny name for a town, isn't it?"

"And then what?"

"Oh, we talk about how long we've had our ticket. That's what we call our license – a ticket, and what sort of equipment we have, and whether we use a ground wire or an antenna. Things like that.

And then we exchange addresses so we can send each other a QSL card."

Doctor Horace was falling behind, and didn't want to ask too many more questions, other than to inquire if she had many cards.

"Sure! A whole wall is covered with them. And I've got a map of the world and put a pin in every place I talk! And, Mother gave me a big map of the whole wide world for my wall, so I put a pin in each city. Mother says it's a wonderful way to learn geology." She giggled. "I guess I mean geography!"

"Fascinating!" Doctor Horace replied, trying to sound interested. The whole idea of tapping out Morse Code to talk to strangers around the world just to mail a post card seemed silly and pointless.

"Oh!" she exclaimed. "I forgot to tell you that's really special. I have one from Eccles. That's where you live! Do you know a Mister Bill Hornaby?"

"Young Bill?" Sure, I know him! He works after school in his father's hardware store. So, young Bill is a radio operator like you? Well, what do you know. Just shows you how you can always learn something new."

"I know! Someday let's send a CQ and see if we can reach him again. It would be fun to tell him you're sitting in my shack."

"Well, we'll see. Maybe. I can't see much point to it. When I get home, if I want to see him I can just walk down to the hardware store. But I'll tell him you're my granddaughter, that's for sure."

Phoebe gave him her best "well, you're no fun" look and quickly changed the subject. "Now, it's your turn Grandfather. Tell me something you about when you went to London. Did you get to see the King?"

He laughed. "No, but I drove passed where he lives. It's called Buckingham Palace. It's a big place. And do you know what his wife does all day while he's working? She dusts and queens!" He laughed at his own joke, but Phoebe didn't understand it. Horace coughed, then continued. "I went for a medical conference where I gave a paper, and that's where I met Doctor Doyle who gave a paper on honey and its medical uses."

"Honey? You mean like what the bees make? It's good for something besides eating? That's a strange thing for doctors to talk about."

"You know, at first that's what I thought, too. It seemed strange to me. But I'm learning more and studying what it can do to help people..." his voice trailed off as he stared out the window, thinking.

"Grandfather, do you mean you have to do homework, too?"

He chuckled and then became quiet again. They sat thinking in silence for a long time. Phoebe brightened up. "I know! You're experimenting with it so you'll feel better and won't have to use a cane anymore!"

"Right you are, girl. Let's remember, this isn't just any old walking stick. This is a special one. Fred found it for me. Let me show you. See, if you unscrew the handle, there's a sword inside. Great for fighting off river pirates and other desperate characters, don't you think?"

Phoebe interrupted him. "We sure could have used that sword last year when we fought off all those river pirates and captured Al Capone's right hand man!"

Doctor Horace laughed. "It might have come in handy then. And that, young lady, is why I carry it with me. You just never know when you might need something like this."

CHAPTER TWO

"Well, this is a surprise! Welcome aboard. From what I gathered from your girl, we didn't think you would get here for another couple of hours," Theo said as he jumped up from his deck chair to greet Harriet. "How did you get away so early?"

"Why, General Balfour, surely you haven't been out of Army Medical Corp so long you've forgotten that rank has its privileges," she smiled, greeting him and Clarice. "Let me guess, Horace and Phoebe are holed up in the library? I'll pop in to say hello to let them know I'm here."

Horace and his granddaughter were so lost in conversation they didn't notice her standing in the doorway. When they did, Phoebe couldn't wait to show her mother the book Horace had given her, pointing out where the author had signed his dedication on the inside cover. Only later did she remember to give her mother a hug.

"I hope you remembered your Paris manners and thanked your grandfather?" Harriet reminded her.

"Yes, Mother," the girl sighed. "Are you home for the afternoon, or do you have to go back out to Ox-Bow?"

"Home to stay. I left early because I knew you were here. Now, why don't you run along so I can have my chance to talk with your grandfather? Maybe Mrs. Garwood could use your help in the gallery." It was more a command than a mere request. Phoebe hurried back to her grandfather to hug him before going out on the deck to start reading her book.

"Lemonade?" Horace offered.

"Only if you don't have something with more of a bite to it hidden away in your secret cabinet," she smiled. "It's been a long day. Well, truth be told, a long summer."

"I think we can manage to scrounge up something. Mind you, my supply is running a little low ever since Theo ran Nitti and his minions out of town. A small one, Harriet?"

"Yes, small, and watered down, too," she smiled. "Now Horace, Clarice said something about you being in the hospital," she hinted.

"Oh, that? Nothing to it really, and I don't think it is a proper subject for a welcome home party, do you? Plenty of time for that later. Besides, I'm doing just fine. And, while we are on the subject of telling tales out of school, your daughter let it slip you're working long and hard at Ox-Bow. She thinks something is worrying you." He lifted up his glass. "Cheers. Is there?"

"You know, you just changed the subject. You never talk much about yourself, Horace. Well, since you asked...."Harriet had barely begun talking about her work when both of them heard the sound of an engine far in the distance. Phoebe burst into the library, "Come quickly, Grandfather. It's a plane. It's beautiful. It's the most beautiful plane ever. You've got to see it before it flies off. Hurry!"

The two of them joined the others on the deck, watching a neon yellow plane circling over the city, then climbing higher to fly over the dunes and back out over the lake. "Barnstormer?" Horace asked. No one answered as they scanned the skies and listened for it. Finally Harriet said, "I doubt it. Anyway, it must have flown off."

The plane was hidden by the trees and dunes, and the sound from the engine faded away as it headed north along the lakeshore. Then, just when they thought it was gone, they could hear it getting closer again. All of them were looking almost straight up or over to the dunes to the west, not realizing the pilot was following the Kalamazoo River, barely skimming over the water, and coming straight at them.

Fred was the first to see it. "Huns! Hun fighters! Coming right out of the sun. Huns! Take cover. Get down men! Take cover!" he shouted as he dived onto the deck and rolled away from the cabin toward the railing, getting as far away from the obvious target of the cabin as possible. Harriet felt Horace's body tense against her shoulder, and saw his face blanch. Both of them were fixed in place, their eyes focused on the plane.

The plane raced toward them, no more than ten feet above the water as it set its course toward Saugatuck, then pulled up sharply just in time to miss crashing into the *Aurora*. It gained altitude and banked to the left over the swing bridge, circling around for another pass, making a victory roll over the Big Pavilion.

"It's all right, Horace," Harriet whispered. "It's all right," she repeated several more times until she felt him relax. "If it is who I think it is, I know the pilot. It's one of the students out at Ox-Bow." They watched as Clarice and Phoebe helped Fred back to his feet.

"Sure brings back the memories, didn't it?" Fred said to no one in particular.

"The old boy's right about that. Bad ones," Horace croaked out. "Imagine, ten years gone by, and it still comes back." By sheer force of will, he collected himself and stood up straight, shoulders back. "Thunderation! Who was that idiot, anyway, flying that low over the city? Could have been a crash that killed us all!" They watched the plane bank again to circle around for another pass, this time wiggle-wagging the wings.

Harriet started laughing and clapping her hands. "Come and see! It is one of my students! I'll show you. Let's go out to the airfield. Come on, everyone." She took Horace's arm to walk with him down the gangplank to the car Fred had just driven off the boat onto the street after his lemonade.

"No wonder you have your hands full, with Lucky Lindy out there painting," Horace muttered in disgust, barking off a final "Thunderation!"

"I'm driving," Harriet announced, and Fred did not object. She shifted the car into gear and pushed down the accelerator, speeding through town, barely making it across the swing bridge before the arm came down so it could open up for a boat. They made it to the airfield just in time to see the plane make a low final pass over the sod to be sure it was safe to land, set down, then taxi toward their car. The pilot unbuckled the safety harness, waiting for the propeller to stop, before climbing out to give a triumphant wave to the reception committee.

Horace's mouth dropped open as the pilot came out of the leather flying helmet and shook out her shoulder length grey hair. "Thunderation! It's a woman! Do you see that? That pilot is a woman! You'd think a woman would have better sense than stunt flying like that!" He pulled his shoulders back, walking stiffly to the plane, ready to tell her exactly what he thought of her exhibition. He took only a dozen or so steps, then froze in his tracks, staring at her.

He turned around to where the others were standing. "I don't believe it! Theo, Clarice, get up here. Do you see who that is? It's Beatrix Howell. I'm sure of it. Tell me if I'm right. It can't be anyone else!"

"Who's Beatrix Howell?" Theo whispered to Clarice. "You think Horace is worse than we thought? Do you know her, or is he confused?"

His wife was worried. "I don't know, but I think he does, or at least thinks he does," Clarice whispered as they watched Horace and the woman walk toward each other, their right hands extended. Clarice breathed a sigh of relief: they seemed to know each other.

"Horace?" they heard her ask. "Horace Balfour? Horace? I can't believe it's you. And I can't believe you're in Saugatuck! After all these years! Is that Theo with you? And Clarice, too?"

Phoebe tugged at her mother's hands. "Mother, what's going on? Does Grandfather know her? How?"

"I haven't the slightest idea, dear, but I do most definitely believe they know each other," Harriet said softly, then walked across the grass to join them. "Horace, Beatrix, you know each other?" she asked.

"Know each other. We practically grew up together! All of us. Clarice, Theo, and me. Years ago, before she became some sort of one woman flying circus and I became a doctor. When did you take up this flying business?"

Oh, three years and two months ago," she said flatly, looking down at the ground. "Back in Minnesota."

"Let me guess, Lindbergh taught you to fly, did he?" he asked.

"No! I would never let that man teach me so much as how to jay walk across a quiet street. He has crashed too many aeroplanes trying to land. The only reason he made it across the Atlantic was because there was no place to crash between New York and Paris. And, the only reason he got his kite down in Paris without busting it to smithereens was pure luck. I would never take lessons from him – ever! Wiley Post gave me my first lesson, and I have been flying ever since."

"Wiley Post taught you how to fly? THE Wiley Post" Horace asked.

"The one and only, old one-eyed Wiley. You see, being blind in one eye means he has terrible depth perception. You might think it is a handicap, but I assure you, it is not. There is nobody better to teach a novice how to land. You either learn or you buy the farm. So, how do you like my plane?"

Before any of them could answer, she continued, rapidly explaining, "It's a Stearman C3, their latest model, thirty-five foot wing span, and I ordered the modified engine with a whole two hundred forty horsepower. That is at least fifteen better than the standard model. She has a six hundred mile range, and more with a tailwind, and all of that with a thousand pound payload, two passengers and a pilot. Can you believe it! And, she will cruise at over a hundred twenty an hour. I left Wold Chamberlain in St. Paul this morning, topped off the tanks in Milwaukee, and here I am! It's exhilarating, and when I am up there I feel free as a bird!" She suddenly looked up again, her eyes flashing with joy.

"St. Paul?" Theo asked.

"Yes, I lie there . I'm a forensic pathologist with a doctorate in chemistry so I teach at the university," Beatrix said.

"And you fly that thing." Horace said, shaking his head slightly.

"All the way across the lake in less than an hour. Imagine. It takes five hours by boat. And now I am spending my two weeks vacation painting at Ox-Bow," she told him.

"Well, would someone PLEASE tell me what is going on? None of this is making any sense," Phoebe stamped her foot as she blurted out in frustration. "Doctor Howell, how do you know my grandfather and my Aunt Clarice and Uncle Theodore?"

Beatrix knelt down so she could look at the girl face to face. "A long time ago, a very long time ago, back when I was a bit younger than you, all of us lived in the same town and went to the same school together. But then, we grew up and went our separate ways. We haven't seen each other for years and years until this very moment."

"But, don't you even send Christmas cards to each other?" the girl asked.

Beatrix stood up, ignoring the question, her voice almost brusque when she said, "I could use some help with my flying bag." She looked at Phoebe, silently beckoning her to come with her, then turned to Harriet to add, "I would not say 'no' to a lift into town."

As soon as Beatrix and Phoebe were out of earshot Harriet said quietly, "Now, Horace, last year, when I first met Beatrix I discovered she is, well, let's just say a little eccentric and shy, and sometimes she seems distant. She talks differently, more precisely and formally. She is a brilliant woman, but, well, I don't know. If you get her started on a subject that she's interested in she can talk a blue streak and be amusing as anything, and then suddenly become withdrawn. I can't explain it better than that. It's just the way she is, so be nice, understood?"

"Don't worry, dear," Clarice said quickly. "We'll keep Horace on a short leash and make sure he behaves. I'm sure you have noticed, but he can be eccentric himself." She sighed, knowing that it wouldn't be long before she would be smoothing over more ruffled feathers. Beatrix would be one more added on to a very lengthy list.

Neither woman saw Horace's lips tighten in a faint smile.

They squeezed into the car, this time with Phoebe sitting on her mother's lap, all of them crowded together. "Why don't we drop some of you off at the boat, and then Fred and I can take Beatrix to her hotel?" Harriet suggested. "Are you staying at the Colonial again this year?"

"I am not staying in town. I am staying at the school. Do you know a Doctor Mason? I rented his cabin. You can take me to the chain ferry and I will walk from there," Beatrix said flatly. "Please," she added quickly.

"Nonsense. No need for that. We'll drive you up in comfort," Horace offered.

"Doctor Howell, do you know what's under the table and carpet in his cabin?" Phoebe asked. Beatrix didn't answer, and Harriet gave her daughter 'that look' making it clear she wasn't to ask a second time. She remained silent until they arrived at the *Aurora* before she offered a quiet, "Thank you for the ride."

On the drive out to the school Harriet suggested, "Why don't you leave your things in the cabin and come back into town with us. You and I could have dinner together and look around a bit. Or, I'm sure Mrs. Garwood would be happy to set a place for you if you would have dinner with us. She always cooks more than we can eat." Beatrix looked past her and said she would be happiest on her own.

"Where's Phoebe?" Harriet asked Horace when she returned from the school and sat down again in the leather chair in his library.

"I gave her some money to treat Theo and Clarice to a Green River," he said.

"You didn't have to do that," she told him. She held up her glass. "Am I falling behind?"

"No. I got lost in reading a medical article. And, I didn't have to do that, I wanted to. I had promised her a treat earlier, but figured if they cleared out of here for a while we could pick up where we left off. You had more you were about to say, I believe."

"Yes. Yes, I suppose I did," she said softly, looking down. "Horace, I'm in over my head. Way over. Mr. Talmadge is out in Virginia talking about a possible commission for a big project I'm not supposed to talk about. I can't really blame him for doing it, because that's how he earns his income. And, the man, Mr. Fursman, who should be running things is in a hospital in Detroit. So, guess who's supposed to ride herd on that three-ringed circus?"

"I don't have to guess. I just hope they increased your salary."

She rewarded him with a withering look of disdain and despair. "That's not the point. I don't even care about the money right now. I know I should, but I don't, and money is the least of my problems. Horace, I'm no manager or director. I'm a teacher. I teach art, not run things. The school board asked me to be the principal, and I said no because I don't want to be a paper-pusher. And the only reason I teach is to pay the bills. But now I'm spending all day going over bills and invoices and authorizing payments. The kitchen, the building, the grounds, payroll. You name it. All of it's paper work. And I hate inventorying paper! I hate it"! There was a frightening flash of anger in her eyes, and her face was tight.

"As if that isn't enough, there's all of this petty stuff happening. Squabbles over nothing. Someone doesn't like the food, someone fusses because there is no electricity, or no telephone. City students who don't like the privies. All of that information was given to them before they registered, but they didn't read it, and then they become unhappy. And, now we've got this petty, stupid vandalism going on. None of it's serious alone, but when it's all pulled together, well, it gets on everyone's nerves. Mine too, especially mine because they want me to fix everything. It's too much, Horace, it is just plain too much! Trust me, I really do understand what Moses went through in the Wilderness!"

Horace watched as she lost her battle fighting against the tears. They ran down her cheeks and she was shaking. He'd seen patients and families break down in tears at the hospital when there was nothing to save a loved one's life.. He'd seen them lash out and rage, kick chairs and tables, or pound their fists against a wall or sometimes even on his chest. It wasn't easy, but he had trained himself not to let it touch him. This was different. It was Harriet this time, and that was what made it far worse.

He sat in silence with her. "Then count me in. If you want my help, you'll have it. Tell me what to do, and we'll get this solved. And if we need to, we will enlist Theo and Clarice."

"That's just one part of it. I'm worried about Phoebe." The tears were flowing freely again.

"What's wrong?" he gasped.

"Nothing really. Maybe it's nothing at all. It's like the pettiness out at Ox-Bow, and oh, I don't know, maybe I'm worried about nothing," she wailed.

"It's a mother's sacred duty to be worried about her children. It's passed on from one generation of mothers to the next. What's she up to?"

"Well, I hate to say it, but it's that radio. And Horace, I'm not blaming you for getting it for her. It was a wonderful gift, and far too expensive for her age, and she loves it. I'm happy for her, and I love you for always being so kind. You might not realize it, but you really are! If she's up in her room tapping out Morse Code, then I don't have to worry about her getting in with the wrong crowd or getting into trouble at school. Or worse. And she has to do her homework before she can use it. But she's in her room ALL the time! She comes home from school, she does her homework, she helps me around the house, and then the next thing I know, she's in her room on the radio."

"Is her school work suffering?"

"Hardly. I almost wish it was so I could make her unplug the radio. She doesn't know it yet, but she's at the head of her class and will be promoted two grades next year. Now, don't tell her that because I'm certain it is a good thing. I haven't agreed to it – yet. She'll be in with older children....."

"I'm not seeing the problem, then."

"Of course, you don't. You wouldn't. Maybe you can 't see it. Horace, she is too much like you. She has a brilliant mind, but she doesn't have any friends. Not real friends, anyway. She doesn't play with the other girls in her class. She doesn't go over to their homes, and she never invites them home. I asked if she would like to join the Girls' Friendly Society at the Episcopal Church, and she wasn't interested. Finally, I told her she had to make a decision – try it for a month or give up her radio for a month. Well, she went, and it lasted for exactly one month, to the day, Horace, because she said all the noise and motion made her jumpy. Honestly, I don't know what to do with that child. She should be out playing and having fun at her age."

"Harriet, the first thing is to settle back. You and I both know she's a wonderful girl. She's interested in the radio right now, that's all. Thunderation! For all we know, after seeing the aeroplane she'll forget all about the radio and want to take up flying. I'm not exaggerating! I wouldn't put it past her this summer to ask Beatrix to give her a flying lesson or two. How does that sound? A year or two from now and you'll come home and find a letter on the kitchen table. 'Gone to see Grandfather. Back in a few days.' Makes the radio seem nice and safe, doesn't it?"

Harriet looked up. The faintest of smiles turned into a grin and the giggles. "You can be so wonderful at times. Not all the time. Just some of the time."

"I don't hear that often. Now, why don't you leave me to think this through? And for heaven's sake, woman, don't you dare tell anyone you think I'm wonderful!"

"I know, it would spoil your image! Don't worry, I'll keep your secret, you old softy." She laughed as she got up to walk to the door. She turned. "Thunderation, yourself!" she shot back him and stuck out her tongue.

"Do get on with yourself, Harriet. I've got some thinking to do, and as Mr. Holmes would say, 'This is a three pipe mystery.'"

He sat in his chair, thinking, letting his pipe go out and relighting it until he ran out of matches. He winced in frustration when he couldn't find any boxes in his desk drawers or cabinets. He got up and put on his boater, moving stiffly across the library until his ankle muscles loosened up. When Mrs. Garwood saw him from the galley window, she sighed, "Squalls and storms ahead." His boater was on straight. At least he had his walking stick with him – this time.

"Fred, I'm going out for a walk to get some matches. Tell Mrs. G I'll be back in time for dinner."

"I can run get matches for you," his driver offered.

"I'm going for a walk to get them – and think. Alone."

"Yes, Sir. Ready to go with you."

"Fred. I said alone. Which part of the word 'alone' don't you understand?"

"Yes, Sir," Fred replied, walking down the gangplank with him as they made their way down Water Street in the direction of Breckinridge's Fish Shanty. He kept his pace slow, not wanting to rush the doctor.

"Say, I'm right sorry about making a fool of myself when that woman, that lady pilot, flew down the river right towards us like that. Brought back what we were up against in France," Fred said quietly.

"Yes. Me too Sergeant. Me too. Sometimes I'm beginning to think we'll never get over it. It comes back to me some nights, especially if there's a thunderstorm. I hear it in the distance, rumbling like a barrage somewhere down the line, and I wake up seeing those boys in the hospital. And when a storm is right overhead overhead......"

"I'm sorta kinda glad to hear you say that, Sir. I thought it was only me that felt that way."

Horace snorted. "Not hardly."

"So, we getting some of that there whitefish while we're out?" Fred changed the subject.

"No, just some fresh air to think things over. And matches."

"Drugstore's the other direction, back behind us, you know. So, you and that fly-girl go back a ways?" Fred asked.

Horace ignored him, turning his attention to a sign in the front window of a house. "Piano 4 Sail. In tune and good shape. Twenty-five bucks."

"Be right back," he said beaming as a fresh idea came to mind. Horace handed Fred a dollar, telling him to go buy some matches. "No need to wait here for me."

"Yes, Sir. I'll be right here."

Ten minutes later Horace was back, smiling.

"You buy yourself a pi-anny? Thought you didn't much care for music?"

"I don't. It's a surprise for the girl, so don't say anything about it when we get back. I don't want to spoil it for her. I think I just solved about one-half of Harriet's worries. Not a bad day's work. Plus, for another five dollars, the fellow agreed to deliver it! And, we'd better turn around and get back for dinner. You get my matches?"

"I'm just about to do just exactly that. I'll walk back to the boat with you, and I'll get your matches and be back in time to put my feet under the table before you," Fred chortled.

At the end of dinner, Doctor Horace tapped his dessert spoon on his water glass to get everyone's attention. "I have an important announcement to make. Well, two announcements, really. Word has come to me that someone or someones, personages as yet unknown, have been creating a bit of misplaced mischief at Ox-Bow. We have a client who has requested our services to track down and apprehend this dastardly villain and put a stop to it."

"Horace, just what are you going on about this time?" Theo asked, his lips tightening

"Quite simply, Harriet said that someone is doing some petty vandalism, and it is disrupting things at school. We're going to look into it and put a stop to it. I thought that was quite clear."

"Clear as mud," Theo muttered under his breath, wincing when his wife kicked him. "And just how are we going to do this?"

"I'm glad you asked. Tomorrow morning the three of us are going incognito to Ox-Bow and sign on as novice amateur painters, learning how to put color on canvas in the fresh air. Officially, we are going out there to paint, which is why we're going to be incognito. Far more importantly, it's to keep our ears and eyes open, and nab this budding gangster in the act."

It was Clarice's chance to puncture his balloon. "Incognito? Three silver-haired novice painters are not exactly going to blend in with the Smart Set, you know. We'll stick out like sore thumbs. You didn't think of that, did you?"

"Ah, but of course I did. I have considered all possibilities, plausibilities, and contingencies. Our friend Beatrix will already be there. Now, she's our age and comes complete with silver hair. And, as I recall from last year, there were several others who weren't exactly 'Bright Young Things' anymore either, out there painting. We'll fit right in. Everyone will think it's just a case of three more old duffers studying art," Horace said in triumph.

"And is our mutual friend in on this hair-brained idea, or did you come up with it all on your own?" Theo asked.

"No. Absolutely not. And, she's not to know, either. This is a top secret mission just among ourselves. It requires secrecy and stealth."

Harriet's mouth hung open.

Phoebe was all smiles, and asked, "Grandfather, I have a question. Have you ever painted before?"

"Well, of course, I have!"

"Oh yes, my big brother was known far and wide for his painting. As long as it was a fence, carriage house, barn, or dog house!" Theo teased. "And, preferably outdoors when he kicked over the paint bucket. After that, he graduated to the Tom Sawyer School of Management."

"Well, I think it's a great idea!" Phoebe answered, rising to her grandfather's defense. "What can I do?"

"Ah, now that's a very good question, young lady, and it brings me to my next point. The job I have in mind for you requires a keen mind, nimble fingers, and well, lots of other things like that. I have a big surprise for you. I think you're well qualified for it. I just bought a piano, and it is going to be delivered here tomorrow so you can learn how to play. You can practice this summer, and if you like it, it's yours for keeps! So, what do you think of that?"

"But I don't know how to play the piano," she objected.

"And that is why I have a lead on a teacher for you."

Harriet stood up, her face flushed. "Horace, your library! Now!" She led the way across the deck.

"I'd say someone just got sent to the principal's office," Theo said quietly. "Can't wait to see how this turns out." He winced when Harriet slammed the door shut. Even with the door closed, everyone could hear her voice but not her words.

"Horace, I realize you are trying to help, but does it ever occur to you, even once, to talk over your plans with me first?" she demanded. "I don't mind you coming out to Ox-Bow to try your hand at painting, but as undercover detectives? When I asked for help all I wanted was for you to listen, not handle it. And maybe, just maybe, offer some ideas or advice. I didn't think you would organize the Balfour Family Detective Agency!"

He was about to say something, but she held up her hand to stop him.

"And, as for this piano idea of yours. Really! You really, I mean, really should have talked with me first. I'm Phoebe's mother, remember? Fine! You bought a piano? Great! Just great! Who's going to pay for the lessons? Who's going to buy the music? Who's going to make her practice when she doesn't feel like it? Did you even think to ask if I wanted a piano in my house? Well? Last year it was the shortwave radio, now it's a piano. What's next? And don't you dare try to be funny by saying you'll get her an aeroplane. Or a car! Absolutely not! Ever!"

"Oh, I'm hardly spoiling her. She's a sensible girl with a good head on her shoulders. Besides, mothers get to worry; grandfathers get to spoil, if your idea of a secondhand piano is spoiling the girl?" he asked quietly.

"I swear, sometimes I can not figure you out. You come up with an idea and charge straight ahead with it. Did it even occur to you that you dislike music, and all summer long she'll be practicing her scales here on the boat. We'll see how you like that!"

The two of them sat in angry silence, trying to say something that would not make matters worse. Very softly he said, "Well, I thought you wanted her to do something other than spend all her time on that radio. Now, if Phoebe learns to play the piano, she can play for sing-songs with her friends in the parlour....."

Harriet's mouth dropped open as she looked at him in disbelief. "Horace, that was half a century ago! You're living in the past! We have indoor plumbing all over town now, and electricity, and automobiles, and radios. Where have you been? People don't stand around a piano singing about riding on a bicycle built for two, or wearing a gray bonnet to go for a buggy ride behind some horse named Old Dobbin, which is a silly name for a horse, anyway. Life's changed even if you haven't.. And, what are you going to say if she wants to play ragtime music, and then ends up as some hussy smoking cigarettes in a speakeasy accompanying some lounge singer? Then what! Honestly, you're impossible."

"Oh, let her try something new and different. Just wait and see what happens. Besides, I won't have to listen to her practicing. I'll be out at Ox-Bow solving a deep, dark mystery," he smiled.

Harriet was not amused. She jumped up from her chair, and marched out of the library. "Thunderation!" she shouted before slamming the door behind her.

In an instant she was back, flashing a sadistic smile. "And, you can find her a teacher, too, since you started this whole mess! Good luck in this town!"

CHAPTER THREE

"Now listen, Horace, it's a nice day, so let's keep it that way. Just be on your best behavior today, would you? Clarice had to do a lot of talking to calm Harriet down last night, and we don't need more of that happening again. So, try not to set her off. And, you might want to start by thanking her for these sketch pads and pencils. Understood?" Theo cautioned his brother. "Just be nice for a change."

"Understood," he said as the three of them got out of the car near the front porch of the Old Inn. "Best behavior. All day."

"Even if it kills you, and that includes Clarice, too," Theo added. "She cleaned up another fine mess you created. I really mean it. Best behavior or else."

They stood by the car, looking around the art school, trying to figure out how to get started. Several students, two of them barefooted, came out of the building, and walked through the rough grass that was still wet from the morning dew, down to the lagoon. "Can't these artists at least put on shoes?" Horace thought to himself. His lips tightened. "They look like refugees from a charity shop," he said under his breath.

His brother shot him a dark look.

A few minutes later they spotted Beatrix quickly walking down the trail from her cabin to the Inn. She obviously saw them, but merely gave a curt "Morning," as she went passed.

"A little frosty this morning, isn't she?" Horace asked.

"Remind you of someone you see in the mirror? Now look, best behavior includes not being sarcastic," Theo said. "Try again, and this time see if you can break your old record of thirty seconds."

"Perhaps she hasn't had her morning coffee yet," Clarice said, trying to smooth things over. Even so, she was surprised at their old friend's demeanor. "Now, what's our plan?"

"Excuse me for interrupting," Fred said. "You want me to stay out here and help, or come back for you later on this afternoon?"

"Well, why don't you go on and then come back later, say around five o'clock or so. I think we'll put in a full day," Horace said. Fred touched the bill of his cap in agreement, then got back in the car.

"Now, I suggest we spread out this morning. That way we can have a full sweep of the field and keep an eye on the buildings. We still don't know exactly what we're looking for, so, until we get a better feel for the place, we won't have any idea what's normal and what isn't around here," Horace said as he doled out the sketch pads and pencils. "That is, unless you two have a better idea."

"Might as well give that a try. Why don't you take your position up here?" Theo asked, pointing to some Adirondack chairs near the porch. "It'll be easier than walking back and forth over that rough ground, and you'll have a good idea of whoever comes in or out the door, and across the meadow, too."

"I won't object to that," Horace said. For once he regretted not bringing his walking stick with him.

"In that case, we'll take the area down near the lagoon. Clarice, if one of us goes over near the dock and the other stays near those little shacks, we can see who's coming or going from either direction. That covers the whole area," Theo continued. "You have a preference for either side, dear?"

"Oh, either is fine with me, but I'd better not catch you drawing any nudes. Remember last year? Besides, we're here to catch criminals, so don't you dare get distracted," she laughingly told her husband.

"All right then, we're set. Let's go to work, and good hunting!" Horace said firmly. He moved over to one of the chairs, sat down, and opened his sketchbook. That was as far as he got. He froze. The idea of drawing seemed simple enough, but only in theory. Doing it was quite another matter, and he didn't have the slightest idea where to start, much less how to do it. He allowed himself to be distracted by watching Theo and Clarice walk across the meadow, choose their spots, and take up their positions. After that, he watched a couple of starlings scout the picnic table and benches in search of morsels left behind from someone's breakfast. Then, someone came out of the Inn, and he watched to see where the woman was going. He soon forgot about drawing.

The screen door slammed again. This time another young man came out. "Hiya, old timer," he said cheerfully. "You're new. Taking up a new career as an artist, huh? I'm Sam. Samuel Dimsdale Witherspoon the third, Harvard. Well, you picked a good spot. Nice chair, shade, and first in line for lunch when they ring the bell. By the way, coffee pot is always on in the kitchen if you get thirsty. Just watch out for the cook if she has a knife in her hands. Privies are over there if you drink too much of it. I'd better get back to my brushes before they dry out. See you in the funny papers, pop."

"Sure. But not if I see you first," Horace said flatly under his breath. He looked down at his sketchpad, still untouched by the pencil. He watched as Sam loped across the meadow into the woods on the other side, then disappeared along the trail by the water. "Now, if something does happen over there, I've got our man," he told himself.

Beatrix was the next to come out of the Inn, carrying a cup of coffee. "Welcome to join me," he offered. She stared blankly at him and said something about having her own work to do, and walked away. He was surprised at her answer. It wasn't angry or unfriendly, just emotionless. But, she had mentioned the magic word, 'coffee,' and he decided that was what he needed. A cup of coffee to help him focus.

The dining hall was empty, but he could hear someone working in the kitchen, out of sight, behind a large cupboard. "Good morning," he said to a thin older woman with short dark hair. "Is there any coffee left?"

She poured him a cup. "New here? You must be or you'd know enough to get your own coffee. I haven't seen you before, so that explains it. Look, I don't mind pouring you your first cup, but from now on you're on your own. You know where to find it. I'm not a waitress in some fancy restaurant, you know. And you clean up after yourself, too. You make a mess, there's a rag in the sink; empties go in that wash tub."

"To the first day, then," he said, toasting her with the cup, forcing a smile despite her tough attitude. "Horace Balfour."

"Roletta Hansen," she said, wiping her hands on her apron. "Roletta Hansen, but if you want to get on my good side, see to it you call me 'Fredericka'. Everyone in town knows me by that name." She blew an errant strand of brown hair out of her face. "It's the female version of Frederick, as in my illustrious ancestor Frederick Chopin. I'm a piano teacher, and keep bees for a living. That's my real work, my calling. This is just a part time job, cooking here. Helping them out, is more like it. I keep my bees out near a big hay-field where there's plenty of sweet white clover. That's what gives my honey its taste – the clover."

She was the very sort of woman that normally would have sent Doctor Horace scurrying out the door. Too much talk, and too fast, but he was in no hurry to get back to drawing. Besides, he knew she could be a good source of information if he could get on her good side. He perched on a stool. "Let me guess. You must like Chopin's music. Have a lot of students, do you?"

"Let's just say I always have room for more. Why? You interested in learning to play the piano?"

"Not really. No, it's an interesting combination of careers you've got, that's all. Beekeeper, piano teacher, and cook." He let out a low whistle of appreciation. It earned him a smile.

"Well, if you do want to learn, I'm the best teacher in the area. And, you ought to know I teach only how to play the real classics. None of this jazz stuff they say is music. It's rubbish. And, I don't believe in arrangements. It's wrong! It's just plain wrong and immoral!" she said with fierceness.

"Arrangements?"

"That's right, arrangements. You heard me. Either music is written for the piano or it isn't. And if it isn't, well, being a purist like my ancestor, I don't believe it is right to play it. It just isn't right. I don't play arrangements, and I don't let my students play arrangements, either. Nor jazz! You want that stuff, then go sit in a speakeasy. That's what I say! You want to learn to play the piano the right way, then I'm your teacher." Perhaps without thinking, she picked up a meat cleaver from the counter, waved it in his direction, and tossed it in an open drawer, closing it with a hard hip bump. Horace winced, thinking of the care with which his surgery team looked after their equipment.

"I take it you teach adults and children?" he asked.

"Yeah. Both. Men, women, children of all ages. Why?"

"Oh, just in case someone comes up to me on the street and asks where they can find a piano teacher," he teased.

"Then, you tell them about me," she said. "Now, I got work to do if you think you're going to get your lunch."

He thanked her for the coffee and was about to return to his chair outside the porch when he thought of new ways to procrastinate a bit longer, this time by making a detour through the lounge. Some of the previous year's paintings were still on display, and there were some new ones. He laughed out loud, thinking of the previous summer when he'd unwillingly bought two of Harriet's paintings, both of them now hanging on his living room walls. The new ones didn't have any appeal, but one painting caught his attention, if only because it seemed very out of place. It was of a reclining young well-fed woman stretched out on her side on a fainting couch, nude except for a whiff of thin gauzy material discreetly draped over her waist and hip. Even to an amateur, it seemed to be in the style of the old Italian masters from the Renaissance. At least that's what he thought. For a while he thought it was a copy, but there were brush strokes of paint that was so cracked from years of exposure he was convinced it had to be old.

It wasn't that he especially cared for the painting, and it was certainly nothing he would ever buy. He didn't even like it, but he was fixated in front of it because it was so different from the rest. The other paintings were in the style of the realists and impressionists, but not this one. He stared at it, trying to understand why it would be there, and so lost in thought he didn't hear Beatrix come through the room. She slowed, then stopped for a moment to look at it. "Interesting," he said to her when he realized she was standing near to him.

"Strange, very strange," she said flatly. He would have asked her more, but she moved on, eager to avoid a conversation. And Horace, not eager to encounter her when she returned, hurried out to his chair to take up his pad and pencil. The coffee had not helped. Just as before, his art career was getting nowhere.

"Lovely sketch of the meadows in the middle of a February blizzard," Beatrix observed without expression as she silently slipped in behind his chair. He didn't know whether to take her seriously or just endure the sarcasm.

"Well, just contemplating for the moment," he fibbed. "You know how it is, waiting for the muse to strike."

She asked for the pad and pencil, spent a few minutes sketching, then returned it to him. "There, that might help you get started. It is rough and preliminary; take it from there, and just draw what you see. The meadow, trees, the shore." He looked at the paper with its rough outline: Two wavy lines for the shore, circles, rectangles, and triangles for the trees, the outline of the gravel road between the spot where he was sitting and the meadow. It didn't seem very helpful. Before he could thank her, she was gone, walking quickly across the meadow, her arms straight down, tight against her body. Horace saw her stride past Theo without saying a word, making her way to an isolated spot farther up the lagoon just beyond the dock.

Still, with just those few lines on the paper, he began drawing, completely forgetting that his real job was to keep watch on the camp and its artists. Before he realized it, he had been steadily drawing for nearly two hours, and was surprised to hear the bell clanging to announce lunch. Horace stood up to stretch, waiting for Theo and Clarice to join him, watching as they met in the middle of the meadow, then held hands as they walked up to him. Such a simple gesture, yet it became the unavoidable invitation for the dark clouds of too many moments of past loneliness to sweep over him.

"How is your new career in art coming? You get the hang of drawing yet?" Theo asked.

Horace squinted against the sun. "You know, I think so. The hard part is getting started. Now, that took me a minute or two, but then once I got going, I did very well. See what you think." He handed him his sketch pad.

"Well, I'll be! Clarice, you know my big brother just might be a real artist. Horace, you keep this up, and one day, say in a few more decades, you might get a job as a medical illustrator," Theo laughed.

"Keep it up, and maybe you can get a job in vaudeville. Let's get something to eat."

They worked their way down the serving line, watching as Roletta Hansen and two young women dutifully and unceremoniously slapped food onto their plates. "I've seen better food at a church basement funeral reception," Horace grumbled as he pushed around some grayish over-boiled vegetables once they were seated at a vacant table near the window. "A stale bun with a piece of cold ham would be better than this." Theo and Clarice sat opposite him, the better to watch who was coming in and out of the door.

"Maybe you'd like Mrs. Garwood to come out to be your personal chef," Theo chided. "Meanwhile, let's remember why we're here. Maybe we'll get lucky and see if we can figure out who is our man."

"Or woman," Clarice reminded them. "Oh, look, there's Beatrix!" She waved at her, motioning for her to come and join them, but she looked through the trio as if they were invisible and moved to a table as far away from the others as possible. The Balfours noticed that no one went over to join her. She was the only person sitting alone.

They watched as their fellow students seemed to linger over their lunch. A table of four young men got into an animated and loud discussion about which contemporary artist was the best. The names meant nothing to Horace. They'd argue and debate, then suddenly lean in to talk quietly, and pull back to laugh when one of them said something the others thought was funny. They continued on, even when some of the more industrious students carried their plates back to the kitchen before returning to work.

The Balfours were about to leave when a young man burst into the dining room, his face flushed with anger, his fist balled up, ready to throw a punch. "All right! Which one of you cretins did it? Who slashed my painting. Come on! Own up! Who? Which one of you thought you could get away with it? Not even a Yalie would be that yellow and low!"

At first there was dead silence, and then several students said that it wasn't them. It didn't calm him, but if anything, made him all the angrier. "Come on, who? Someone got a beef with me we can settle it out in back, one on one right now. Or are you too yellow to fess up!"

Horace recognized a woman from the previous summer, Sylvia Mueller, get up from her table and go over to him. "Sam, that will do! Go see Mrs. Walters," she told him softly. "And calm down. Being angry and wanting to throw a punch won't help. That's enough of that. It's only going to make everyone upset. Now, go see Mrs. Waters and tell her what happened." She took hold of his shoulders to turn him toward the door, giving him a gentle push to move.

"Yeah? And just what will she do? Nothing! I'll settle it my way."

"Go. Now," she told him softly but firmly.

"You know him?" Theo asked his brother.

"No, not really. We spoke briefly this morning, and he seemed like a nice enough fellow. Samuel Dimsdale Witherspoon, I think he said," Horace whispered.

"Harvard man, I take it?" Theo asked.

"Right the first time." Horace smiled. "Samuel Dimsdale Witherspoon the third, by the way."

"Anyway, it looks like the vandal struck again," Clarice said softly. "I thought everyone was in here having lunch. He came in after us, so who could have done it? Looks like we haven't gotten anywhere, have we?"

"Well?" Horace asked.

"Well what?" Harriet demanded, her face flushed.

"For starters, what did Sam say?"

Harriet relaxed ever so slightly. She let out a long sigh of frustration. "Sam said he came in for lunch with everyone else, and told me that his painting was up on the easel. He had lunch, went back out, and it was slashed and the stretcher broken. That's about it. Do you know where he was working?"

"Not precisely. He walked across the meadow and went toward the trees in front of the lagoon, near the boat dock," Horace told her. He regretted not keeping closer tabs on him.

"Well, did anyone come in for lunch after him?" Harriet asked.

"Beatrix. Well, at least she was the last one to come in the dining hall. But I don't know if she was the last one to come into the building. She came in by herself, if that's any help."

"You see what I'm up against. I'd better talk to her...."she blew the air out of her cheeks in frustration. "That's not going to be easy, but maybe she saw something. I don't know."

"You want Clarice to talk with her? She's good at that sort of thing."

"No, that's something I have to do, but thank you. My job," she said. "I'd almost rather do more paperwork than face her."

"All right. I told Fred to come back out about five. We'll scout around a bit more until then," Horace offered. "Maybe..... well, I don't know."

"There's not much point in that, Horace. We only get one of these events a day."

"Always at noon?"

Harriet snorted in derision. "I wish. Then we'd have a possibility of catching someone in the act. No. That's the problem. It's never the same time, never the same place, never the same type of vandalism. It's random and always something different every time. Look, if you want a ride back into town early, you could catch up with Mrs. Hansen. If the pattern holds, we've had our mischief for today. She'll be leaving before long. A couple of hired girls do the washing up. Meanwhile, I've got to talk with Beatrix."

"You must be one of those Sunday afternoon painters," Mrs. Hansen said sharply when Horace wandered into the kitchen. "I don't see you actually doing much work. I suppose you're dilly-dallying by wanting another cup of coffee. Well, help yourself. It's that or water. If it's something stronger you want, I don't supply it. It's against the law, you know. So, none of that funny business filling up a hip flask in my kitchen," she said, waving a dirty knife in his direction.

"Why, I wouldn't dream of such a thing," Horace smiled. It struck him as a bit odd that she immediately hinted at bootleg alcohol.

"See to it that you don't around here. Laws are made to be obeyed, not broken, not that it seems to matter to some people. Well, go on then, help yourself. That's John Reynolds," she told him, pointing a large knife in the direction a youngish man leaning against the counter. "He looks after things around here."

Reynolds mumbled a quiet 'hi-ya' and took a loud slurp of his coffee.

"Caretaker, huh?" Horace asked, forcing a smile. "You know, my old father used to say that it's as important to get to know the janitors and cooks at school as it was to get on the good side of the principal. I think he was right. You're the folks that know how things run. I'm glad to meet you." He put out his right hand to shake hands with him.

"I don't hear that often around here," Reynolds said, beginning to warm up a little.

"Well, that's only what I think. I guess others see things differently. Too bad for them, and for you. Say, that was some dust-up at lunch. Happen often?" Horace asked.

"Ah, someone's being nasty. Mischief mostly, if you want to know what I think. Most of them that come out here haven't done a day's work in the their life, so they think they'll become an artist. Take that fellow Sam, you know, the one whose painting got ruined? Always introduces himself like he's a real swell. College boys! And then, when they figure out they can't cut the mustard as a painter, much less real work, they make a little mischief. They want to stir things up, I guess. Anyways, that's what I think, even if Mrs. Walters wouldn't tell you that," Reynolds said with contempt. He stood up, rinsed out his cup and put his it in the sink, then sauntered out the back door of the kitchen. Realizing he had probably said too much, he added, "Well, she wants to be encouraging, I guess."

Mrs. Hansen interrupted. "Now, what have you decided about learning the piano?

"I was just going to talk to you about that. Now, you told me you teach children? Beginners, I hope." He asked her. She said she did.

He smiled and continued, "I've been thinking it over. I'm only here during the summer, but my granddaughter lives here year round. I think learning the piano would be a good thing for her, and she's old enough to learn."

"You heard my rules," she interrupted. "Same thing goes for children. She'll practice and learn to play right, and no arrangements. Chopin didn't write arrangements, and I don't play them. She won't, either, as long as she is my student, is that clear? She got a piano?"

"As a matter of fact, I bought one for her yesterday," he smiled.

"Say, you move right along, don't you? No moss growing on you. Well, good for you. You got yourself a piano and a teacher. All righty-right, I'm finishing up here and from what I can tell, you're wasting your time out here, even if it's none of my business. Tell you what, I'll give you a ride back into town and we'll see the piano and the girl. Ten minutes. Meet me at the truck out in back."

Horace left a note on Harriet's desk, telling her that the three of them were going back to town, and he hoped she would come for dinner. He turned to leave, then went back to the desk to add, "Please come. Important. Big surprise!" He left her office with a surprisingly big smile across his face.

Captain Garwood spotted the truck pull up to the side of the *Aurora* and watched as Clarice got out of the cab and dusted herself off. Horace and Theo had ridden in the back and were brushing bits of hay or straw out of their hair and off their clothes. "I'll bet that brings back memories of your boyhood," Clarice teased.

"It's a highly over-rated experience," Horace growled at her.

"Boss, you order a piano?" the captain shouted down from the deck. "Some fellow just brought it here, and he and Fred got it aboard and shifted it into the lounge. Fred said you bought it yesterday. They pulling my leg or something?"

"Capital!" Horace clapped his hands. "Is Phoebe here?"

"Last I saw her she was bouncing up and down all over the place, and doing the two-step on the walls and the waltz on the ceiling. She wanted to know if that thing is for her? 'Must be,' I told her. I can't imagine you'd get it for yourself."

"Yes, of course it's for her. See if you can find her so she can meet her teacher."

Before Captain Garwood could turn around, Phoebe brushed past him to race down the gangplank, her arms wide open to wrap around her grandfather. Once again, any aspiration toward her mother's interpretation for the girl to learn Paris Manners was completely forgotten. "Thank you! Thank you, Grandfather! I've always wanted a piano, but Mother always just said, 'we'll see.' Thank you!"

"Phoebe, I'd like you to meet your new teacher, Mrs. Hansen."

The two looked at each other, Phoebe's eyes widening with fear commonly associated with getting a vaccine injection or a semi-annual visit to a dentist

"I know you," Mrs. Hansen's voice was sharp and unpleasant. "You're Mrs. Walter's girl, now aren't you? Never mind. Yes, I know who you are. I've seen you out to Ox-Bow and around town." She turned to Doctor Balfour and said, "You didn't tell me you and Mrs. Walters are related."

"I didn't think of it," he admitted. "Frankly, I didn't think it mattered."

"Well, never mind. I s'pose it don't matter none who's your family. It's just that I like to know these things, see. Who I'm dealing with, and things like that, understand? Never mind. Let's see this piano. You ready for your first lesson?"

Phoebe quickly calculated her initial wariness of Mrs. Hansen against having her long desire to have a piano and a teacher. She breathed and relaxed. "Yes! Yes, please! Can we really do it today, even if we don't have any music?"

"We won't need music today. I'll show you the keyboard and learn you how to hold your hands and your first scale. When you get that down pat we'll get some music. Or, maybe you'll be a natural at it, and just play by ear."

Phoebe looked at her, taking Mrs. Hansen literally, and wondering if she would have to bounce the side of her head up and down the keyboard.

Horace, Theo, and Clarice stood discreetly in the doorway as Phoebe sat down on the bench. In rapid-fire orders, Mrs Hansen made her sit up straight. "Now, put your hands on the keyboard." She moved Phoebe's right hand slightly to the left, pressing down her thumb to strike a key. "That's Middle C. You gotta remember that one. Play it again. A couple more times. Get the sound of it in your head. Now, use your pointer finger on your right hand.

"Now arch your fingers like they are a barn. That's it. Nice and arched up. Gotta make room for the animals. Keep them arched up or you'll crush all the animals in the barn. Good. Now, you're going to play your first scale." Mrs. Hansen turned around to her audience. "I don't need no supervision. You three scat!"

"That's quite the racket out there," Theo said a few minutes later when he and Clarice came into Horace's library. "Quite the lively place this summer. Piano student and detective agency. What do you have in mind next?"

"Close the door behind you. Thunderation! That girl is hitting nothing but sour notes. It's absolutely painful! You two want some liquid painkiller? And you're right, we made a poor showing of it out at Ox-Bow, I'd say." He turned around to open his cabinet, then turned back to Horace and Clarice holding up a fresh bottle. "At least Fred's been successful!" He poured them each a generous two fingers of Scotch.

"I've been thinking the same thing, too, about this morning," Horace continued. "We didn't come close to catching the vandal, and frankly, I don't see how we can unless it is by pure dumb luck. Even with the three of us out there, watching everything, it's going to be next to impossible to keep track of everyone all the time. Look what happened at lunch. We let down our guard for a minute or two, and it happened again. And not a hint at who might be doing it.

"And from what Harriet said, it never happens at the same time or place twice. It's too random. One day it's in the morning, another time in the evening; today it was at noon. We'd have to be out there around the clock, keeping watch on everyone and everything," Theo added. "We're spread too thin now as it is. I don't know...." his voice drifted off. "And never the same thing, either."

The three of them sat in silence, thinking it over, hoping to find an answer. "I was just thinking," Clarice began. "Today it was that painter. Sam, I think you said that his name, whose painting was slashed. Now, just hear me out, but what if he didn't like the way it was going, and took a knife to it himself? He got rid of a painting and shifted the blame to someone or something else. You said he was working by himself, so maybe he did it before lunch, came in and ate, then went back out afterwards, and came in again worked up and ready to fight. But what if he destroyed it himself?"

Theo nodded in agreement as his wife continued. "Some of the women from our literary society dabble at paintings, and I've heard mention of how artists sometimes get so frustrated they do that sort of thing. So... maybe?"

Theo and Horace looked at her, their eyebrows rising almost in unison. "To tell you the truth, I hadn't thought of that," Theo said.

"And, maybe he's not the only whose done something like that. Harriet said it is all petty, minor stuff. Nothing major. Thunderation! It could be anyone. Why, it could have been Mrs. Hansen, for all we know. We didn't keep an eye on her. She could have slipped out the kitchen door and done it. She's just the type, too," Horace added. "I've seen that women wave knives around in the kitchen. Maybe that isn't the only place."

"And I take it that is the same Mrs. Hansen who is teaching your granddaughter how to play the piano, is it?" Theo teased.

Horace rested his head in his hands, ignoring his brother's sarcasm. "That's my point! It could be anyone. Harriet, for that matter. You know how some of the boys with shell shock could be a bit peculiar. Well, Harriet's been under a lot of pressure, so maybe she's cracking up, if you want to follow that line of thinking, which I certainly don't!" Horace said. "We're going to get loopy ourselves if we start chasing down that road."

They lapsed into silence again until Horace whispered, "Listen!"

"What? I don't hear anything," Clarice said.

A smile slipped across Horace's face. "That's right. We don't hear anything!" He pulled himself to his feet and hurried to catch up with Mrs Hansen who was still on the deck. Theo and Clarice followed him, going back to their cabin.

"We never talked about your fee for teaching Phoebe," he reminded Mrs. Hansen.

"I get a dollar a lesson," she said firmly, holding out her left hand. "That's top dollar because I'm worth it. And, I get paid up front. I don't give credit to nobody no matter who they are."

He gave her a five dollar bill. "That's for today and the next four lessons."

"You're taking a chance doing that, you know. If she quits on me, I don't give refunds."

Horace grinned at her. "Well, I've never been the sporting sort of man, but I'm more than willing to take chances when it comes to my granddaughter. She'll follow through, so don't you worry. I certainly won't. She comes from good stock. Say, what else do you know about that fellow Sam? We started talking and then got interrupted."

"Sam? You mean that young fellow whose picture was knifed? Not much. He's been out here since the first part of June. Nice enough young man, as far as I can tell. Good manners, seeing as how he probably was born with a silver spoon in his mouth. Probably comes from too much money for his own good, but I guess he can't help that, and if he does at least he doesn't put on airs, if you know what I mean. He's a decent enough painter, but he'll never be a Charlie Russell. Now, there's a man who knows how to put the paint on canvas. When he paints something it's aces."

"Say, I'll bet you know Beatrix, too," Horace asked.

Mrs. Hansen raised her eyebrows. "That one? Her? She's a strange woman. She might be a real lady, but she's just too quiet for my tastes. Keeps to herself. She came up last year early in the season and spent a week. Real snooty, if you want to hear what I think. She comes in for meals and eats by herself, and then goes out to work on a painting. I heard someone say she's a doctor. Well, that's no job for a woman, if you want my opinion. Why are you asking? You sweet on her or something?" she teased.

"No, just curious. I ran across her in the main lounge once or twice," Horace said.

"Uh-huh, I see," she said sarcastically.

He watched as she walked down the gangplank to get in her truck. A wave of exhaustion swept over him, and he was eager to get back to his study and sit down, and soon napping with his head on his desk.

He awoke with a start, a fist rapping on the door and hearing his name being shouted. Harriet didn't bother to wait for an invitation to come into the library. "I was just down at Bird's Drugstore, and you'll never guess who I ran into. No, maybe you would know since she was just here this afternoon. Roletta Hansen, all smug and sweet, telling me you had just hired her to teach my daughter how to play the piano! Is that right? Did you? Tell me you didn't."

"Yes," he said.

"Do you even know anything about her?" she demanded.

"Well, I know she's your cook out at the school, so I assumed that she would be all right."

"And, what else?"

"Well, she lives just out of town. Like I just said, she cooks at Ox-Bow, raises bees, and teaches the piano. And, she seems to have some rather firm ideas... "

Harriet's eyes widened. "Well, I'm quite sure you think that's sufficient knowledge about someone to entrust my daughter to her.

But let me tell you something. That woman is certifiably insane. She's completely crazy. She isn't just sprinkled in pixie dust, she's rolled in it. She should be in a padded cell. For all I know, maybe she was, and somehow broke out and escaped because they used cheap locks or someone forgot to lock the door. Yes, I know she is our cook, but that's not my choice. The woman shouldn't be let anywhere sharp knives. I wouldn't trust her with a butter knife, if I had my druthers, and I don't trust her around my daughter!

"As for her cooking, let me tell you. She told me her mother taught her everything she knows about cooking, and her mother was called the 'Village Poisoner' for good reason. Two years ago we had a Halloween party at the church, and she brought small cakes. Fine. Except they were pumpkin cakes with dill pickle icing! I thought it was a trick at first because it was Halloween, but she said, and mind you, said it with a straight face, she thought they were very tasty. Besides, it was a way to finish off a pickle jar. No telling how many years that jar had been on her shelves."

Horace was about to say something, but Harriet held up her hand to stop him.

"At least she comes by it naturally. Years ago her mother brought some preserves to a church sale. Do you have any idea what they were? She'd found some bright red berries on their property. If it hadn't been for May Francis Heath, they would have killed someone because they were pokeberries. Pokeberry preserves! Quarts of them. Not pints like most people would bring, like normal women, but quarts. There was enough of them to kill off everyone in Saugatuck and half of Douglas. Mrs. Heath got rid of them in a hurry!"

"Well....." Horace tried saying.

"Now, as if being the daughter of the village poisoner isn't enough, her name is Roletta Hansen, but she thinks, no, she really believes, she is the reincarnation of Frederick Chopin, and wants everyone to call her Fredericka. I won't do it, and I don't want you to start, either. And this, this, is the woman, the crazy lady, the insane woman you hired to teach my daughter!" Harriet collapsed back in her chair in exhaustion.

Doctor Balfour stared at her for a few seconds and said softly, "Well, from what I've seen around here, she seems to fit right in. She's just a little more eccentric than others."

"Eccentric? Are you serious? The woman needs to be locked up!"

"Harriet, slow down and breathe. I'll grant you, she is definitely an odd one, but Phoebe's lessons are here on the boat, and we'll make sure that when Mrs. Hansen, or whatever she wants to be called, is here, someone will be around to chaperone and keep an eye on her. And, I'll tell Mrs. Garwood to make sure she keeps the knives locked up, and not let Phoebe eat anything she brings. And, I'll talk with Phoebe, so don't worry. Everything will be fine. She's a sensible girl. You raised her, after all."

She still wasn't mollified. "Horace, I don't know what sort of medical problem you had last month, but I swear, it's addled your brain." Harriet knew she had gone too far when she saw the pained look on his face. She gasped and quickly apologized.

Horace glared at her. "And what I want to know why, if she is as deranged as you say, she's working as your cook?

"Because Mr. Fursman hired her and she signed a contract, so I can't fire her. And, she's done nothing to justify firing her other than her reputation for being crazy. He gets to make those decisions, not me, so that's why!" She got up and marched out of the library, leaving the door open. Almost immediately she wheeled around. "Oh, and what a surprise, three more of your friends have turned up!" She stepped aside so the guests could enter. "And by the way, since you've suddenly become so fond of surprises, here's one for you. I invited Beatrix to join us for dinner! She'll be sitting next to you."

"Say, we saw your boat is in town, and hear some piano music when we were walking past a while ago. We thought we'd come calling. Don't tell me you became a music lover, Doc?" Trix Justus teased.

"Not yet. By the way, I thought Theo hired you to direct the park band back home. What are you doing over here?" Horace growled.

"Don't you worry. I've got this young fellow who plays the sax, and he's good, real good, one of the best. He's a music major at DePaul University over in Chicago and wants to be a director, so I've let him rehearse the band once in a while. I told him it was time to quit rehearsing and just do it. Don't worry, I'm paying him out of my pocket, so it's not going to cost you boys anything. Let's just say you might have a big hand in giving a young man a break. Now, you remember Ollie Anderson and his Blackhawk Orchestra from last year, up from *Aurora*. Well, they're playing for a week at the Big Pavilion, so I'm sitting in with the horns. And this here is Les Stoddard, best piano player you've ever heard."

"Good to see you again, Mr. Anderson," Horace told him.

The short man waved at Doctor Balfour. "Mind if I give your piano a test drive?" Les asked. Without waiting, he led the group into the lounge and sat down at the bench. He ran his fingers over the keys a couple of times. "Nice, real nice. Good action and good sound. She's got a good feel to her."

The sound of the piano brought Phoebe scurrying into the lounge. "Gentlemen, my granddaughter, Phoebe. I believe we ought to ask her if it's all right to play. It's her piano, after all."

"Well, Little Sister, jake with you?" Les asked. "You have a favourite piece you'd like to hear?"

"Oh, yes please! Do you know 'Old King Tut?'" she asked.

"So, you like the old stuff do you?" Les laughed. "Sing along if you know the words." He played the tune twice, with Phoebe singing the chorus and pretending she was an ancient Egyptian. When he brought the piece to an end he continued calling out one popular song after another, finally ending with 'Nola'. He might have continued, but Harriet returned, and very politely and firmly suggested that was enough music for one day. "Say, I can give you lessons, if you like, Little Sister," he told Phoebe. "You'd be playing rags in no time," he offered as he closed the cover. He looked up at Harriet, "You, too, sister." An icy stare from her mother, and Phoebe knew the time had come to thank him and tell him she already had a teacher.

"You girls get tired of that long-haired stuff...." his voice trailed off when Harriet gave him "that look" that mothers normally reserve for errant young children. He didn't finish his sentence.

After the trio left, Harriet let out a long sigh and looked up to the ceiling. "Compared to having jazz musicians around here, well, I'm not saying I like it, but maybe we should see how things go with Mrs. Hansen. For just a week, one week, period, and then we'll decide."

Phoebe steeled herself against jumping up and down in joy, and swallowed quickly to give her mother a heartfelt 'thank you'.

Horace would have found it easier if the three musicians had stayed on for dinner. If nothing else, they made a lively diversion and seemed to constantly know how to have fun. He would never admit it, but he envied them. Fun was always something that eluded him ever since he was a boy. Beatrix was the opposite of the musicians. She was stiff, formal, and tightly polite. She hardly spoke, even when someone asked her a question, and then answered with as few carefully chosen words as possible. When she did talk, she rarely looked at the person, or anyone else, for that matter. To add to it, over dinner, Horace noticed she had her own special ritual. She carefully separated her food so that it was not touching anything else. She took one small bite, then set down her fork for several seconds, eating each serving in rotation, turning the plate counter-clockwise. Far worse, she refused an offer of ice cream. That was the great and unforgiveable sin, not wanting ice cream, as far as Horace was concerned. There was something suspicious about anyone who didn't share his enthusiasm for ice cream.

Still trying to make some sort of connection and be a gracious host, he asked. "Care to see my library?" he asked when the meal was over. She said 'yes', stood up and followed behind him.

"Comfortable. Neatly cluttered. I expected that of you. This is where you escape, obviously," she said flatly as she looked around. She lifted a medical article off a chair so she could sit down, looking at the title. "Doctor Nigel Poole's article on royal jelly. It is not marked, so you have not read it yet. You should. It is quite informative, although with more anecdotal examples than I would have preferred. Is this because you know Roletta Hansen is a bee keeper?"

"No, just a new interest of mine," he said.

"I am surprised she did not tell you that by now that she is an apiculturalist. The woman constantly talks. What surprises me even more is that you did not observe it from the stings on her hand. The two of them on the right hand are recent. They are probably from this morning. The one on her left wrist is older." She looked away and lapsed back into silence, slowly studying his bookshelves.

"Now, I may be wrong. You got the idea about royal jelly from reading Sherlock Holmes, did you not?"

"Well....."

She smiled wanly. "That explains the pipe too, perhaps. Then again, men of your age always preferred pipes. You were always older than you seemed, even when we were growing up." She looked at him again. "Little professor. I remember, now. That is what people called you. You were teased about that. I was called the same thing and found it very painful. Well, I must be going. Harriet said she would take me back out to Ox-Bow."

Horace was still in his library when Harriet returned. "All right, Doctor Balfour, you infernal reprobate. You won that one, even if it was just sheer luck that those musicians turned up in time to pull your irons out of the fire. Mrs. Hansen can stay on, at least for the time being. You opened Pandora's Box bringing that piano here. I'd rather she learned from her than that jazz pianist. I don't think they are a good influence on her. But please, just listen to me, if something involves Ox-Bow or Phoebe, would you talk with me first?"

"I'll do my best," he said softly.

"I assume Phoebe is in her cabin and asleep by now?" When Horace nodded she said, "Well, time for me to go home, too. And no sitting up half the night reading for you. Bed."

Horace rolled his eyes and mockingly let out a long sigh, "Yes, Mother."

"You're incorrigible," she laughed. "Bed. Sleep. I need you bright eyed and bushy-tailed in the morning so you can catch my vandal."

CHAPTER FOUR

Doctor Horace paused to look at a notice on the sign board near the door to the porch at the Old Inn. "Art Show & Sale. Thurs, 5 to 9 PM."

"You thinking about putting something in the exhibition, or will it start past your bedtime, Gramps?" a young woman asked, turning her violently red lips into a smile that was more of a smirk. She was the very sort of woman Horace instantly detested. She was one of those bright young things with bobbed hair and make-up. He was about to say something when Beatrix slipped up behind him and said, "Ignore her. She has obviously had a very poor upbringing to be so rude. A regular little Clara Bow and Gloria Swanson all rolled into one. But then, so am I. Rude, I mean. I did not thank you for dinner last night." She paused and added "Thank you."

"You're welcome. I hope you'll come again." He was about to ask if she was going to put something in the show, but she had already moved toward the kitchen for a cup of coffee. He had also been on his way there, and as much as he wanted a cup, he decided to wait until later, rather than trail after her. Instead, he wandered into the lounge to look at the old painting again. He could sense there was something odd, almost off-putting about it, and it had captured his attention. He couldn't put his finger on it, and consoled himself by muttering that he was no expert. When he saw Beatrix leaving the building he got his coffee and returned to his drawing.

"Say, Gramps, maybe you need something to help you loosen up," the same irritating young woman he had met earlier said to him. Before he could answer, she pulled up a mid-length black skirt high enough to retrieve a flask from her stockings. She held it up. "Bath tub stuff, but it's got a nice kick to it, with a little sweetener. Do you a world of good," she offered. He declined, and she shrugged her shoulders. "Change your mind, and just ask around for Paulette. Everyone knows me," she giggled. Horace didn't doubt that for a second.

The young artist looked over to the far edge of the meadow where Beatrix was standing at her easel. "Your girlfriend is the type who could use a few bumps. She's as cold-blooded as they come. Bet she's a hit woman for Capone. What do you think? She could whack someone without batting an eye and go right back to painting."

"In that case, I don't think it would be wise to interrupt her," he said gravely.

"Sure thing, Gramps, sure thing. Just wanted to be friendly and liven things up out here. Your loss, not mine." She started to walk away, turned around, and curtsied to him, giggling. She started singing "Charleston, Charleston" and dancing as she went away.

"Barely morning and she's already tipsy," Horace muttered under his breath.

Once again, noon came far sooner than he had expected, and Doctor Horace jumped at the sound of the bell. "You two go on it. I'll join you up when I'm finished," he told Theo and Clarice when they arrived at the porch of Old Inn. "Almost done." They all knew it was a ruse, allowing him to wait until everyone else had come in first, scanning the meadow to be sure no one was trailing behind.

"When you get in, why don't you take a different table so we can keep a better eye on everyone?" Theo suggested. Horace nodded in agreement.

Harriet came in and joined Horace, and a few moments later, when Beatrix was carrying her food to a table, she waved her over.

To her surprise, Beatrix gave a half smile and joined them, remaining as emotionally distant as ever. It didn't look like she was even going to speak to them, but Horace wasn't giving up.

"I was thinking back to something you said about Wiley Post teaching you how to fly..." he said, hoping to usher in a warmer breeze. "How did you make that happen?"

Beatrix was distant at first. "Mr. Post is a good friend of one of the surgeons, and when he came up to the university hospital he left his plane at Wold-Chamberlain. When he was ready to leave he asked if I would drive him back to the airfield. When we got there, Mr. Post asked if I had ever been up in an aeroplane. I had not, of course, and he asked if I wanted to see the Twin Cities from the air. We went up, and then he told me to take the stick. I did, and I have been flying ever since. The Stearman I have now is my second plane."

"You're second?" Clarice asked.

"Yes," Beatrix replied. "My first was a well-used Army surplus trainer, a Curtis, without the guns, thank you very much. It was already long in the tooth and far too slow for me. That is why I bought the C-3."

"And Wiley Post taught you how to fly? I am impressed," Horace said.

"It is the truth, but only in a sense. It is not the whole story. Mr. Post taught me how to fly a plane. I had another instructor who taught me how to land and take off. That is the hard part."

"The hard part!" Horace laughed loudly. "Now that has to be an understatement!" He laughed again. "And what about doing those loops and flying upside down and other stunts? How did you learn those?"

"I took lessons," she said quietly. "I admire Mr. Post. There is a man who knows how to fly for adventure, but he does not do stunt flying. I took lessons from another instructor for that. I can take you up late this afternoon if the weather holds and show you why I enjoy it." She smiled, then added, "If you also are a man of adventure, that is." It was as much a dare as an offer.

"I, I, well, I'll take it into consideration," Horace said cautiously. He didn't see Harriet squint and look sideways at her friend for a rather wicked combination of offering a dare and a bit of flirting at the same time. That was absolutely the last thing she expected of Beatrix. And, she smiled again when she realized that, as usual, Horace was oblivious to it.

Harriet was enjoying his discomfort, and pushed her luck, "Oh, I think you should, Horace. Really! It would be quite the experience to go up in a plane with Beatrix It might be your last opportunity."

"That's sort of what I'm afraid of, my first and last flight."

Their conversation was interrupted when John Reynolds, the caretaker, burst into the dining hall. "Hey! Listen up," he shouted. "Listen up, everyone! Quiet! Pipe down! It's starting to sprinkle. You got your stuff outside, now's the time to get it in before it rains. Let's go! Move! Now! Let's get going!"

There was a brief moment of silence while the students absorbed the news, followed by shouting, the scraping of chairs on the floor, and a stampede for the door. A few plates and utensils clanged as they hit the floor, with at least one plate shattering. Beatrix moved as quickly as the artists a third her age, outpacing several of the young men as she made a dash across the meadow to gather up her supplies. Like the others, she was soaked long before she returned.

Theo and Clarice came over to Horace's table. "Glad we put our things in the shack down at the lagoon," Theo smiled. Horace told them his sketchpad was on a shelf in the lounge, then decided he should move it away from the screened windows.

The students began trooping back into the Old Inn, shaking and brushing water out of their hair and off their clothes, staking out places to resume work. Mrs. Hansen told them they could not use her dining room, but everyone seemed to ignore her. She shouted her instructions a second time, stamping her left foot in fury. Tables were pushed to one side, chairs stacked and piled one on top of the other. And in the midst of it, Paulette was making the rounds offering what she was touting as a bump of "anti-freeze" for two bits. A few of the students apparently were quite chilly, and took her up on her offer.

"It is loud and I do not like being in a crowd," Beatrix said as she stood near the three Balfours. "I am going back to the cabin and read."

"I'm through for the day, too. I hope Fred knows it's raining and will come out to get us. I think I'll catch up on my reading. Look Beatrix, we were all up to Doctor Mason's cottage last year, and it is a stretch to even call it a shack. It's rustic as anything. You're welcome to come back to the boat and read. It'll be more comfortable."

"I am going to read," she repeated, firmly.

"That's fine, just so long as you don't read out loud," he told her. He reminded again her he also intended to read.

"What my big brother is trying to say in his uniquely charming way is that when he reads he doesn't want to listen to a lot of chatter," Theo apologized for Horace's rudeness.

"The article in Lancet I saw last evening?" Beatrix asked.

"Yes, I thought I would."

"In that case, I will accept your invitation. I would like to look at it again when you are done, and then perhaps we can discuss its merits."

"I think you and I are about the same size," Clarice said. "I'll be happy to lend you some dry clothes," she told Beatrix. "When you get on board, just go down to Phoebe's cabin. I have an outfit or two there. Mrs. Garwood will help you if you have questions. " To her surprise, Beatrix suddenly looked rather alarmed. Clarice quickly added, "Or, you'll probably be dry by the time Fred gets us back there." She watched Beatrix relax again.

The four of them didn't talk much on the drive back to the boat, and as they were getting out of the car Fred asked if he could drive up to Holland for a haircut. "What's wrong with Dominic's just down the street?" Horace asked. Fred told him it had more to do with seeing some old army buddies than anything else.

"You have finished reading this, I take it. Well, what did you think of it?" Horace asked Beatrix.

"Interesting. It may have possibilities for cognitive improvement in geriatrics. There is more testing to be done." Beatrix noticed that she had caught Horace's interest. "Did you happen to notice the co-author's name? Beatrix Bronwyn Morgana Howell." She flashed one of her rare broad smiles. "I have been researching royal jelly for the past three years. I am convinced there really are potential benefits, but not what your Arthur Conan Doyle tells in his fiction. It is no fountain of youth, and yet it does seem to strengthen the brain, especially in older people where the acids can aid in expanding the capillaries. Expansion leads to more blood flow, and more blood flow leads to more oxygen getting into the brain which should, I hope, mean better brain function. I would be satisfied if it had measurable positive effects on mental clarity. That will require additional testing, using a control group or double-blind testing.

"Concentrating sufficient royal jelly for more widespread testing is the real challenge, and I believe it has to be concentrated to be effective. Otherwise, it is just a sweet tasting nostrum," Beatrix told him."

"Side effects?" Horace asked.

"For anyone allergic to bee stings, it can be fatal. Horace, tell me why this so interests you. It is not a pure academic study, is it? You have a deeply personal interest in this that borders on the obsessive."

It was an intimidating question that would force him to reveal more of himself that he wanted to give away to a woman who was almost a complete stranger. He said nothing, and was relieved when Fred knocked on his study door and let himself in.

"I thought I'd better let you know I'm back, Doc," his driver said.

"I trust you had a good time. Say, it doesn't look like the barber got too close to your hair with the scissors," Horace teased.

"Well now, you're sorta kinda right about that. I went to have Charlie cut my hair up to Holland, and he said I looked pretty sharp the way I was. I didn't see much point on spending money I didn't need to, so he took me over to the Warm Friends Tavern to say hello to some of the fellows Doctor Theo and I met last year. They were right pleased to see me again, and some of the boys wanted you to have this gift on account of what you did to them Bolos last year. Charlie said that if you'd like to, they'll make you an honorary Polar Bear any time. Right decent of 'em, if you were to ask me."

"Well, that's a surprise. You know, you ought to ask Theo about going up there with you. Now, what's the special gift?"

"Well, it's a box of cigars that ought to be pretty good on account of the fact they left the price tag on the box and there's twenty five of 'em at a dime each. And, this thing here." Fred held up a hand grenade. "Now, don't worry on account of the fact that it's not loaded. One of the fellows got hold of some dummy grenades that sort of fell off the truck over by the armoury, if you get my meaning, and made 'em into cigar lighters. It's a trick lighter, too!"

"Trick, huh? How does it work?" Horace asked.

"Now, with a regular grenade you squeeze down on the little lever to pull out the pin. You let go of the handle and toss it. Now, with this one, the trick is to pull out the pin and then squeeze the lever to make it light. You do it in complete reverse."

"Well, that's something, isn't it? It sure is something," Horace said.

"I told the boys that it'd be a big hit with you, and say, I guess I'm right! Say, you two were talking. I didn't mean to barge in like that."

As soon as Fred left the room, Horace let out a long sigh. "I could open up a second hand store with all the useless trinkets he brings back here. Well, do help yourself to a cigar," he offered. She said nothing and returned to reading the Sherlock Holmes story.

"Before you say even one word, I know very well that this is pork and not whitefish. I was at the store and the butcher gave me a very good deal on a pork roast, so that's what I cooked, and that's what I'm serving, and that's what you're going to eat tonight. Waste not want not, and that includes money, even if it is your money. Now, eat it up, or you'll be having it tomorrow night!" Mrs. Garwood said firmly.

Doctor Horace leaned over to Fred to whisper, "I don't care what's going on tomorrow. Your job is to drive Mrs. Garwood to the first fish shack you see, and make sure she buys whitefish. And, if for some fool reason they don't have it there, go to the next one! Just don't come back without some." Fred just nodded in acknowledgement.

Clarice had noticed the look on Horace's face, glared at him, and then turned to Phoebe to change the subject. "Tell me about your piano lesson? What did you learn today? And, are you still liking it?"

The girl instantly brightened up, knowing that adults had invited her to be part of the dinner conversation. Sometimes it seemed as if they almost forgot she was there. "Well, I practiced my C scale, and I did okay until some of the wrong keys kept getting in the way of my fingers. And, I learned the G major scale. And, I learned that the black keys are sharps and flats, but they change when you go up or down the scale, and Mrs. Hansen hasn't explained that to me and I can't figure it out. And, Mrs. Hansen said I had to learn how to use both hands at the same time which is really hard."

"That is just wonderful dear," Harriet told her daughter. "You know, Horace, I think you are wonderful buying her that piano. You've got the entire summer to listen to her make such wonderful progress." She had a sadistic smile on her face, knowing that every clinker and sour note rankled him.

Phoebe wasn't finished. "And, I want to learn as fast as I can so I'm going to practice an extra hour every day so I can become a real piano player like that man who was here yesterday. You know, Mr. Stoddard. He plays such fun music. I think he's wonderful."

"I don't think so, dear," Harriet said. "Mrs. Hansen wants you to play proper music, not jazz, and I agree with her on that." She looked over her glasses at her daughter with 'that look,' to emphasize the point.

"Meanwhile," Harriet continued. "Thursday night there is an exhibition and sale at Ox-Bow, and a chance to show and sell your work. Or, buy yourself some more paintings. I trust that sounds interesting to you, because we can always use some additional guests."

Theo and Clarice said they would come, but they really weren't good enough to exhibit anything unless it was to be hung upside down in an outside privy. Beatrix quietly said she had two paintings to show, but didn't know that she wanted to part with them, and wouldn't sell them. "Well, that leaves you, Horace? What about you?" Harriet asked.

He looked thoughtfully at her. "Now, of course, last year I bought paintings, so this year, I might try selling. Yes, you know, yes, I think I will put mine up for sale. A young woman student, I think her name is Paulette, told me that my drawing of the meadow was a fine example of ultra-primitive abstract folk art, almost childlike in its rendering, with a definite nod of appreciation to the minimalist tradition as well as the Obstructionists all at the same time," he proudly announced.

The others were silent for a moment or two, not quite certain what to make of his description. Harriet had a look of pure horror. Clarice and Beatrix had to look down at their plates and use their napkins to suppress their giggles. Theo just shook his head and said, "You surprise us all, Horace." Phoebe looked confused, and Fred said, "Say, boss, if no one else buys it, maybe that would be a fine gift for the fellows up to Holland."

"From what my brother just said, you'd better check first to see if they want to hang them in the restroom. Now, Harriet, what surprises me is that you hold this show on a Thursday night," Theo said."I would have thought Fridays would be better."

"Friday would be worse. It's just the opposite. On Friday evenings, everyone wants to go to the Big Pavilion for the music and dancing. No one would ever come up to Ox-Bow. Trust me, we learned that lesson the hard way. That's why we do it on Thursday."

"Can I come, too?" Phoebe asked. "And, if I come with you out to Ox-Bow on Thursday, then maybe we can all go to hear the music the next night. I'd really, really, really like to hear Mr. Stoddard again." She emphasized the point by singing a chorus of "Old King Tut."

"See what you've started with those friends of yours," Harriet grimaced. "My daughter is becoming a flapper!"

"Can I?"

"Yes, but only for a little while, and only if you practice your scales."

In a flash, without remembering to ask to be excused from the table, Phoebe stood up and dashed to her piano. The wrong notes made both Horace and Beatrix wince in pain.

It wasn't long after that their guest said, "I think I should go back now. Could I trouble someone for a ride? Or I can take the chain ferry and walk back from there?"

Fred quickly offered to take her back. "I think I'll come along for the ride," Horace said. "That girl can sure hit all the bum notes. Maybe she'll get the hang of it by the time we get back. You mind taking the scenic route out there, say through Chicago?"

They were about to leave when Harriet hurried down the gangplank and joined them in the car. "Thanks. I didn't realize how badly she plays. Why don't we take the scenic route through Chicago and come back the same way?"

It was after Beatrix had been dropped off that Harriet admitted to Horace why she came along. It had nothing to do with Phoebe's practicing. "We had more vandalism this afternoon," she barely whispered.

"What was it this time?" he asked.

"One of the students needed something from the store room, and told me the legs of three new easels had been broken. Ruined."

"Thunderation! We should have stayed around to keep an eye on everyone. I thought with all of them being in the building.....We should have stayed," Horace said.

"I doubt it would have helped. Besides, it might have happened long before this afternoon. I talked to everyone before coming home and asked if anyone had been down to the storeroom earlier in the day, or seen anything suspicious. Nothing. No one saw or heard a thing. I even talked to the students who had packed it in for the day and went to have a nap. I hoped that they might know something. Nothing. And, of course, they're all worried they'll be next, and getting suspicious of each other. You could cut the tension with a knife. Why? Why is someone doing this, Horace? Not just why, but who, and what can they possibly be getting out of it?"

"Fred, drive along the lakeshore road for a while," Horace said. He turned back to Harriet. "I hate even saying this, but I saw something that didn't make any sense. I made a point of being the last one to come in for lunch. Theo and Clarice were watching the front and door and doors, and they didn't see anyone looking like they were doing anything suspicious. But, here's the thing. Beatrix came in ahead of me, but then she was lagging behind and was the last one to come into the dining hall for lunch."

"You think....?" Harriet asked.

"I'm not thinking. I am only telling you what I observed, not making a diagnosis. It's the only thing that seemed out of the ordinary. And, now that I think about it, I'm not certain it is out of the ordinary. She hangs back from everyone all of the time and never mixes in."

Harriet thought through Horace's observations. "It's terrible. Everyone is so suspicious of everyone else right now. They're all on edge. This afternoon after it happened, Sylvia and Cora told me that they and a couple of other women from town are thinking about not coming out any more until it settles down. They said they could paint in town at their own homes. I don't want that to happen. Not to them; they're friends. And, I owe it to them because they helped out when I was on my own with Phoebe. Besides, there's never been a close relationship between the people in town and the school. This will only make it worse."

"Just hold on tight. We'll find out who's behind this," Horace tried to reassure her.

They rode on in silence, both thinking and trying to find an answer. Horace didn't say it, but Beatrix wasn't the only unusual person out there. There was also Paulette. Enough bath tub gin from her flask and she might lose whatever inhibitions she had left, and think it was a fun prank to break things. Or, Sam, the big friendly painter from Harvard. What if all of that was a mask for something dark and destructive? And there were probably others, too.

"Penny for your thoughts?" Harriet asked when Fred pulled up to the boat.

Horace chuckled. "Not worth even a penny."

DEATH BY PALLET KNIFE

CHAPTER FIVE

Horace did not sleep well that night, waking up, turning everything over in his mind, and finding it impossible to stay asleep. It was all such petty mischief and vandalism, and that troubled him. It was the pettiness more than anything else because it was senseless. Someone was taking incredible risks, possibly ruining their reputation, maybe even risking arrest, and all of it for a sadistic fling. It didn't make rhyme or reason.

He had experienced it in the past, and for a while he thought about those experiences. There had been the young nurse who was caught stealing small items from the hospital. A roll of bandages one time, tongue depressors another, gowns and gloves. When she was finally caught and the police investigated, her apartment was full of things she'd taken from the hospital and nearby stores. She told the officers she just liked collecting them and having them. Since she wasn't stealing them to sell, Doctor Horace hadn't pressed charges when she agreed to enter the state hospital for treatment for her kleptomania. She wasn't the only one like that he'd encountered. There had been an older woman in Eccles, years earlier, just after electricity was installed, who stole light bulbs from stores, claiming that they were instruments of the devil. Every month or so her son would drive down from Thief River Falls to return them to their rightful owners, and then the cycle began again. Everyone understood that she was just an eccentric old woman, harmless, and they watched over her.

During the war there had been young privates, and even a corporal or two, who broke and busted up things, the result of shell shock, or hoping to get a medical discharge and be sent home. Most of them needed a furlough to calm their nerves. At least that was understandable under the strain of two weeks or more in the trenches. It would be for anyone on the front for very long. Another orderly, in a field hospital up the line, had pilfered everything he could find to sell to a French unit. He had thousands of dollars rolled up in his duffle bag. Or, at least that was the story.

And there were always youngsters, usually a small gang or two or three, who misbehaved. They might soap windows, or throw eggs at a house, or let the air out of car tires. One little group would put fresh horse manure in a bag, set it on fire, then ring the doorbell and hide in the bushes as the owner came out, saw the fire, and stamped it out – with the inevitable result clinging to their shoes. They were bored, probably badly treated at home, or trying to stir up some excitement or take out their frustrations in life. Maybe, what they really wanted was the thrill of getting away with something. All of it harmless really, even if the town cop didn't see it that way. Perhaps that was happening at Ox-Bow: thrill seekers. He'd already discovered that it was far more fun to think about painting or drawing, than to do the work. It was a triumph to have completed a piece. It was that middle part, the work itself, that was hard going and exhausting. Maybe, that was it. The work was hard, they needed something to pump some life into their day or further distract them.

Contented with that conclusion, he finally drifted off to bed an hour or two before sunrise.

When he finally roused himself and went up to the lounge for breakfast, everyone but Theo was gone. "Clarice went out to Ox-Bow with Harriet about half an hour ago. I don't know why. It had started raining earlier. I told her there wasn't much sense in it, but she said something about wanting to give Harriet some moral support. Phoebe is still asleep, and Fred took Mrs. G to buy some fish."

"Well, it is a good morning, then," Horace yawned, pouring himself a cup of coffee. "No sour notes and a reasonable and holy hope of finally getting some whitefish for dinner."

"You going sour on the girl?" Theo asked.

"No! Of course not! Not on my Phoebe. Just all those sour notes she hits. Much more of that and I'm going to have Captain Garwood take us out in the lake and bury that confounded piano at sea. Anyway I'm glad you are here." Over their coffee he told Theo about his conversation with Harriet from the night before, and his sleepless night.

Theo nodded. "It's been on my mind all night, too. I was thinking earlier about something you said when that phony minister was murdered last year. You said that murder always makes sense, if only to the person who did it. Well, that didn't make good sense to me at the time, but it did later. What if it applies to this situation, as well? I know, it's not murder, but still...It doesn't make sense to anyone other than the person doing it."

Horace's eyebrows shot up in interest. "Go on, then."

"Well, maybe we should do what we did last year – chart it all out."

"I understand that, Theo, but let's face facts. We didn't solve anything last year. All we did was sail straight into an ambush like the rank amateurs we are, and we got out of it by sheer dumb luck," Horace said softly. "Much as I hate to admit it."

Theo said slowly, "I know we did. But then, when we got into a jam, we improvised, remember? Fireworks, and I'll never forget the look on Harriet's face when she blew up their run-about with a flare gun."

"That's what I mean. We charted out everything and couldn't come up with an answer, and if we had, it would have been the wrong one. It's just pure dumb luck we didn't get ourselves killed. Don't forget, Nitti got the drop on you with his finger in your back. Even Harriet's shot was a one in a million."

"Yeah, all right, all right, and you don't need to remind me about Nitti, but maybe this time will be different. This time we'll get the jump on them." Theo stood up to get paper and pens from the library. On the way out he spotted the school's roster on Horace's desk and brought it along. "If we can see a pattern, we have a chance.

"So, we start by crossing off the names of all the students who came up here this week. Since the mischief started before they got here, it isn't likely to be any of them," Theo said as he started removing names.

"And, we can exclude the locals like Sylvia, Louise, Mrs. Ruley, Cora Bliss."

Horace interrupted. "No, we can't."

"Why? Why not?

"Just because they're a local doesn't mean that they can't be the culprit. Look, for all we know, one of them, maybe all of them, have got some sort of squabble going on. I'll grant you, they all seem nice enough in public, but we don't know what they're like in private. What if it's something that goes back a generation or so. They could have their claws out for each other just waiting for the right minute to pounce We don't know. It could be anything – jealousy, rivalry, malicious gossip, you name it. Maybe it goes all the way back to their mothers having a tiff. So, no, I don't think they can be excluded. Not yet anyway. So, the way I see it, it could be any one of them."

Theo looked at his brother, remembering how their mother never had a nice thing to say about Miss Jensen because years earlier her mother had broken a serving plate. She never let go of it until her dying day. Theo nodded in agreement, and the names stayed on the list. He worked in silence, Horace impatiently sitting across from him.

"I hate to tell you this, but you're forgetting something else. We're assuming it is someone connected with Ox-Bow. Well, what if it's someone outside the school doing it? Maybe someone up to the Presbyterian Camp who slips through the woods, does something, and goes back unnoticed. Could be a mean-spirited game they're playing, or a dare. Or, maybe someone from the town who just doesn't like the school? Harriet said that not everyone in town likes a bunch of artists out here. So...." his voice trailed off.

"That's a bit of a stretch, don't you think? I see what you're saying, though. Sort of takes us back to the beginning of not knowing who or why."

"Thunderation!" Horace growled.

The two men sat in silence, looking in opposite directions, off into the distance, neither of them noticing that Fred had been standing at the door. "Sorry for interrupting you, but I couldn't help but overhear what you were saying, especially seeing as how I was listening in. Can I say something? I had the idea that maybe it isn't just one person, but a copy-cat. First man does a bit of mischief, and then someone gets the idea they ought to give it a try, too, if you don't mind me saying what's on my mind."

"You realize, don't you, that you just made it all the more complicated?" Horace asked. He pounded his first on the table with a loud, "Thunderation!"

"No, of course not. It's a possibility," Theo countered, then asked, "Is it still raining?"

"Naw. Quit raining a while back. Drizzle's just about done, too," he said.

"I wouldn't eat the biscuits if I were you," one of the students said. "Old sour puss used salt instead of sugar. She said someone switched the canisters around."

Horace nodded in acknowledgement, and the two brothers went into Harriet's office. "More vandalism, I hear."

"Yes," Harriet sighed. "I thought maybe Mrs. Hansen had made the mistake, but someone poured all the salt into the sugar container, and the sugar into the salt. It was no accident. And, someone took the pins from the door hinges in one of the studios. My guess is that they're at the bottom of the lagoon, which means I have to send John in to Koening's Hardware to get new ones. No one seems to know anything, again, of course." She sighed a second time, trying to fight back tears.

"It was raining most of the night, so maybe they did their dirty work inside to avoid leaving foot prints. You have to hand it to them for thinking," Horace said.

Harriet ignored his comment. "Any ideas? Helpful ones?"

"Yes," Theo told her. "We were just talking about how it might be someone from outside the school. Well, if there aren't footprints, we can rule that out. It's someone here."

"That's helpful, I guess. Maybe," Harriet admitted. "Anything else."

"Just one. I'm going to take a different approach. I'm going to quit trying to pretend I'm an artist, and let people know I'm a newspaper man or a magazine story writer, out here to do a story. That way I can move around more easily, talk to people, and keep my eyes open. So, if anyone asks, I'm writing a magazine piece about Ox-Bow. People can't resist talking about themselves if they think they'll be famous," Horace said.

"You know which magazine you're writing for?" Theo asked.

"Oh, we'll say it's the Saturday Evening Post. Everyone's heard of it."

"Sure, and now you're a writer up there with Fitzgerald, are you?"

"Don't you get smart with me. I know what I'm doing. People love talking about themselves. You know how quiet Beatrix is? Well, ask her a question about flying or medicine, and she's a regular Dan Patch at the starting gate. So, maybe one of them will talk too much."

Harriet and Theo watched Horace walk off toward the lagoon, pen and a pad of paper in hand. "And there he goes, Horace Balfour, ace reporter," Theo joked.

"Be nice. He's really trying to help." Then she giggled. "I was thinking of Lowell Thomas tracking off across the Arabian Desert in search of Lawrence of Arabia."

Horace spent the next hour or so watching the artists, talking with them, making some notes when they told him about their work, and asking how they spelled their names. Word soon got around, and he had one person come up to him after another. He'd ask, talk, ask more questions, and always slip in a question or two about the mischief. If he wasn't making any immediate progress, at least he felt he was accomplishing something by getting them to talk. It would come in useful in the future.

"I need to talk with you, Horace," Beatrix said firmly when she came up to him. "Over there on that bench."

"I have been thinking about you. Neither you nor your brother and his wife have said what happened that put you in the hospital. From what I have observed, you are favouring your right leg and using a cane, but there is no physical evidence of a stroke because the right side of your face is symmetrical and you are not weak on your right arm and hand. I observed you writing, and your fine motor skills are quite good.

"Well, I really don't want to get into that," Horace said.

"I understand. But I have noticed your interest in royal jelly. Obsessively so, as I told you the other evening."

"You're rather obsessed with it, too, you know."

"That is because I am doing clinical research. You are not. I doubt you had any interest in it until you spent time with Conan Doyle and the topic came up. That tells me you are anxious about something you do not wish to discuss," she said flatly.

"That's right. I don't wish to discuss it."

"I believe I could help you, but I must know what happened. Do not worry, what ever you tell me will be in confidence. I will not be talking to Theodore or Clarice, if that is what concerns you."

Horace thought for a full minute, and winched up his face. "It's rather embarrassing. I was hit by a car when I got off the 'L' in Chicago."

"That is hardly a cause for embarrassment," she said.

"No, perhaps not. Except that I had just come back to the States from being in London where they drive on the wrong side of the road. I looked the wrong direction. For a moment I forgot I was back in the States," he said slowly. "I forgot where I was."

He had expected her to make light of it. Instead, she sat silently staring off toward the lagoon. "I understand," she said slowly. "For a moment you forgot where you were, perhaps thinking you were still in England where, I am sure, you rode the street cars on occasion while you were there, and quite naturally you looked to the right rather than the left. You were there long enough for it to make an imprint on your brain. You were hit by a car, and now you are concerned you are beginning to lose your memory. Am I correct?"

"Well done, Doctor," he said sadly. "Yes," he barely whispered. "Right the first time."

"Which in turn led you to remember your conversations with Doctor Doyle about royal jelly, and that led to your interest in the article in the Lancet."

"Yes."

"I see. I believe I can help. Is Fred still here?" she asked. She looked up to the Old Inn and answered her own question. "Yes. May I borrow him to go into town?"

"Of course, but what are you doing?" Horace asked.

"I will be back in a couple of hours." She said, walking briskly up the meadow.

On the whole, that evening's exhibition and sale didn't seem to have much going for it. Harriet had gone out early to help set up and boost the morale of her students. Phoebe came out a bit later with the rest of her family, and within a few minutes was excessively bored and would have welcomed a chance to go home. It wasn't very interesting for a young girl, and when she found an old upright piano in a lounge, she asked her mother if she could practice her scales. Harriet was quite nice about it, but the answer was a firm and decisive 'no'. The evening was already tense without having to endure a youngster practicing.

Some of the local amateur artists, the ones Harriet called "Sunday-afternoon painters," were the first to arrive to see what the students had been doing. They looked at each piece, sometimes commenting or saying something encouraging to the artist. Others, friends and family members, most of them locals, came out. Some of them were decidedly bored. They looked around at the work on display in the lounge and on the porch, saying all the right encouraging things. In time, they came out to look at the art on easels on the lawn. They finished looking at the exhibition and wandered across the meadow to the lagoon where a few students were still painting.

Phoebe and a young woman about her age came out of the Old Inn, letting the screen door slam behind them. Curiously, each of them was holding several pieces of bread. "Better not let Mrs. Garwood see you with that," Clarice told her. "She'll be upset because she'll think you didn't get enough for dinner."

"Oh, it's not for us, Aunt Clarice. We're going down to the canoe dock to feed the fish and turtles!" she answered as the two of them hurried down to the water's edge.

It was very obvious that the artists were staying close to their work, keeping an eye on it, hoping if the vandal, made a cameo appearance, their presence would lead him or her to find an easier target. Even Horace could sense the tension and wariness in the air. No one was more tense than Harriet, who was trying to be casual and relaxed as she talked with people, but was forever looking around, preoccupied with her fear of what might happen.

Theo and Horace chose to meander around the grounds, looking for anything out of the ordinary, or seeing someone acting suspiciously. "Too many people around for anyone to try some funny business," Horace observed. When Fred and Clarice joined them, they also said they hadn't seen anything unusual.

"In that case, I'm going back up to the Inn and sit down on the swing," Horace told them. "I've been on my feet a lot today."

He was mildly irritated that the swing was already taken, but found a couple of wooden chairs in front of the building. He sat down to enjoy his pipe. The air was still, and he was just far away from everyone else to enjoy the view of the lagoon through a thick tangle of brush and trees. The relative solitude and being left alone relaxed him.

"I thought you had to be somewhere nearby. I could smell your pipe. Mind if I join you? The smoke keeps away the mosquitoes," Beatrix said, then sat down without waiting for an invitation. They sat in silence until Horace asked, "You accomplished your errands, I take it?"

"Yes. I asked Fred to take me to Parrish's Drugstore, and the pharmacist was quite helpful. And, then a telephone call back home. I asked that some Royal Jelly be sent here immediately. It should arrive in a day or so. Meantime, I have sufficient to spare." She handed him a small glass jar. Take two now; then two more tomorrow morning."

"Now?" Horace asked. She didn't answer.

Beatrix got up and brought him a glass of lemonade. She watched, like a tough old hospital ward nurse with an errant patient, as he took two pills and finished the drink.

"You should feel a sharpness of brain function in a few minutes," she told him before sliding back into silence. Horace liked the silence, and it gave him more opportunity to watch people.

They were interrupted a dozen or so minutes later when John the caretaker came by, turned back to them, and paused. "Quiet evening and no wind. What say I build a little campfire down by the canoe launch? We could sit around and have an old-fashioned sing-song, if you like. I've got a uke. Sound like fun?"

"I do not sing," Beatrix told him, her face expressionless.

"Well, let's give it a whirl. I don't sing too well, either. We'll be the audience," Horace suggested. "Might be a fun way to end the evening."

John touched the trim of his hat with a couple of fingers, adding that he'd start the fire after some of the guests had gone home. He was about to move on when Horace stopped him. "Say, as long as you're here, John, what do you know about that old painting in the lounge? The old one..."

"You know, now that's a real puzzler. A couple of months back, just when we were getting ready to open up the place, I found the painting all wrapped up, leaning against the front door one morning. It was just wrapped up in butcher's paper and baling twine. No name, no address, no nothing. I showed it to the powers that be around here, and they didn't know much about it. I figured I'd just hang it up on the wall in the lounge." He shrugged his shoulders.

"That seems highly irregular," Beatrix said.

"That's what I thought at first, but this isn't the most regular sort of place, either, so I keep my nose out of things and just do what I'm told," John smiled.

Doctor Horace took a long draw on his pipe, thinking it over. "Yes," he answered slowly, "I suppose you're right. Everything always seems a bit casual around here, doesn't it?"

John chuckled, "And I just do what I'm told. It's easier that way, don't you think?"

They might have remained seated where they were if Sam and two of his friends hadn't come out of the Old Inn carrying a Victrola and a stack of records. "Hey, put in a new needle! I just got those records. I don't want them ruined." Sam snapped at one of the young artists. "Open the door. Needles are in the box, and make sure you change them every time you put on a new record."

Paulette came up to join them, her silver flask in her right hand. "You got 'I Wanna Be Loved by You' because I really, really wanna be loved by you, Sammy," she flirted. She took a sip from the flash and handed it around to the others.

"Seems like a good time to leave," Horace said quietly to Beatrix. She nodded in agreement.

It was late in the evening when John struck a match to the twigs and pine cones he had set in the fire pit, gradually adding larger pieces of wood to build up the first. Phoebe joined Beatrix and her grandfather to walk across the meadow down to the small sandy beach. Coming from the trail that led to the Crow's Nest were the Garwoods. It was twilight before Theo and Clarice, trailed by Fred and Harriet, joined them. By then the fire was burning brightly, and Clarice was fussing that whereever she sat the smoke seemed to drift her way. "Of course it does, dear. Why, you draw everyone and everything close to you," Theo teased.

"Shsss, you'll make me blush," she giggled.

"Too bad it's dark, then," he countered back.

For a while they watched the fire, following the trail of sparks upward every time the wood crackled and popped.

"John, I thought you were going to lead us in a sing-song," Horace reminded him.

"Say, that's right. I'd better run back to get my ukulele from my cabin. I think I know where I left it!" He got up and loped across the grass into the darkness.

"I don't sing," Beatrix said, repeating herself.

"I'm no Caruso myself, and Horace is worse, so don't let that bother you," Theo said.

Apparently it did bother her. Beatrix stood up, and without a word, walked down to the shore, turning left to go along the beach. Minutes passed before she returned.

"Sorry it took so long, but I had to put a new string on. And, then when I saw how dark it had gotten I got a lantern to put on the table. When you're ready to go up, just walk towards the light and you'll be right in front of the Inn," He tuned his instrument, strummed the strings several times, and was ready.

"We should have borrowed the Victrola. Did anyone hear Paulette sing? She knows ALL the new songs," Phoebe blurted out.

"I'm quite sure she does," Harriet said icily. "I think the old songs are better for a campfire, don't you, John?"

"You're the boss. How about 'Beautiful Ohio'? John played it through once, and then they joined in. And from there, they rolled from one song to another until the fire began to die down. Clarice saw Phoebe failing to stifle some yawns and said, "I think you've got the right idea, dear. It is getting late for all of us."Everyone seemed to agree, but John continued with one final song, "The end of a perfect day." They sat in silence, realizing it had been a perfect day that was now coming to an end. Eventually, they got up to make their way back to the cars.

"You folks go on ahead. Like I said, just walk straight cross the meadow toward the lantern. I'm going to throw some water and sand on the fire. Folks, thank you for making it a memorable evening," John told them. All of them thanked him for the campfire and music.

Horace was stiff and unsteady on his feet as they started out. "Just take your time, Grandpa," Phoebe said solemnly, holding his hand. She yawned and said, "Uncle Theo and Aunt Clarice won't leave without us."

The darkness was pierced by a shout of surprise. It was Clarice's voice.

"What's wrong?" Horace shouted.

"It's okay. I just tripped on....." She let out a loud scream.

"What?"

"Horace, get a move on! There's someone on the ground!" Theo shouted.

"Who?"

"I don't know. It's pitch black here. Hurry up!" Theo shouted to his brother. "Fred! Fred! Get the car and drive down here. We need some light. Someone's fallen and I think they're hurt. They're out cold!

"Harriet, go up to the Inn and bring down some lanterns or flashlights, anything you find, and bring them back here as fast as you can."

Horace, Beatrix, and Phoebe, and then the Garwoods came through the dark, barely able to see Theo and Clarice kneeling next to the person on the ground. When Fred brought the car closer and trained the headlights on them, they could see what they were doing.

It appeared to be a man, lying face down on the ground. "Looks like he tripped on something," Theo said.

"Or had too much to drink and passed out," Clarice said as her husband searched for a pulse. Horace joined him, pressing his fingers against the carotid artery in his neck. The two brothers looked up at each other, both saying, "Nothing."

Harriet had found some lanterns and was hurrying across the meadow with them as Horace told Clarice, "Take the girl up to the Inn and stay with her. This is no place for a child."

"I want to see," Phoebe wailed.

"Be quiet, girl! Do as you're told. Clarice, take her up to the Inn," Horace snapped. They waited a few seconds as Clarice took her by the hand, practically dragging her away. When they were gone, the two men rolled the man over, revealing a large dark red stain on the left side of his white shirt." All of them gasped, staring at a knife buried in the wound.

"That looks like a palette knife!" Harriet blurted out.

"A what?" Theo asked.

"A palette knife. Artists sometimes use one to spread paint on a canvas instead of a brush. It's like a little trowel," Beatrix explained.

"That's a palette knife, alright," John said when he joined them on the ground.

Fred and Theo helped his brother to his feet, and he gratefully took his walking stick from Beatrix. "All right," Horace said quietly, taking charge of the situation. "Fred, you take Phoebe, Clarice, and the Garwoods back to the boat. Tell them to stay there. No wandering off. And tell Captain Garwood he is to keep watch. Now Fred, listen, when you get there, I want you to find my revolver in the top right hand drawer of my desk, and bring me another pouch of tobacco. And more matches. After that, go find the police chief and tell him that there's been a death out here, and he's needed right away. Nothing more. Just a death, understand? Don't say someone was murdered, understood? Someone died. That's all.

And then you get back out here as quickly as you can. You got all that, sergeant?"

Fred pulled himself to attention and saluted. "Yes, Sir."

"Good man. Get moving. You've got important work to do. Now Harriet, go up with Fred and explain things to Clarice, and after they're gone, come on back down here. And don't worry. Phoebe will be just fine with the Garwoods and Clarice. You'll be needed here when the police come."

She had her hand over her mouth, and just nodded.

"What do you want me to do?" Beatrix. "I may be some help."

When Theo and Horace paused to look at each other she said firmly, "I have seen bodies before. I am a pathologist, after all."

"Yes. Yes, of course you are," Horace said quickly. "Yes, we can use you. Stay here with us. Right now, we need to keep everyone as far away from here as possible. Off the meadow. Keep everyone off the grass. John, go up there and stop anyone from coming any closer."

"I can do that," he answered. "I'll just say there's been some sort of an accident if they ask." He took one of the lanterns and jogged up the meadow in anticipation of curious on-lookers. This sort of news would spread through the campus in no time. Even those who had turned in for the night would be coming to see what happened.

When Clarice had gone to the Inn and John was out of earshot, Beatrix said quietly. "He wasn't killed by that palette knife." When the brothers didn't respond, she repeated her observation.

"I'll see if I can find a bench or chair or something," Theo said, then walked toward the Inn.

Horace flinched as he felt Beatrix' hand brush against his. She handed him two more pills. "For focus. It's going to be a long night. Can you swallow them without water?"

CHAPTER SIX

Fred returned within the hour; the police chief half an hour later, and with an apology: "Sorry about not getting here sooner. A few of our young visitors were mixing it up outside the Pavilion. A combination of a little too much to drink and a disagreement about a girl. We get that once in a while, and I don't want it getting out of hand." He put out his right hand to greet the Balfours. "Ed Garrison, police chief. I'll be taking charge of things."

Horace made the introductions. "We've already met," the chief said when Harriet was introduced. "Harriet Walters, the chief warden out here, right?"

"I'm one of the teachers; informally, I'm the temporary director," she explained.

"Wish it was under better circumstances," he said when he met Beatrix. "And I already know about you two. Chief Callie told me about last summer when you got the Capone mob out of town. Not that they've exactly stayed out, but they keep quiet. So, what have we got here? Anyone know the victim's name?"

"No, but I can tell you he's not from the school. I haven't seen him before," Harriet said. No one else knew him, either.

"Any reason you can think of why he'd be out here wandering around at night?"

"We had an exhibition and sale, you know, something of an open house, earlier this evening. It's a way of introducing the local residents and tourists to the school. I don't recall seeing him, but he might have come out here for that."

"That happen often, these open houses?" the chief asked.

"Every Thursday during the summer," Harriet said.

"And none of the rest of you recognize him from around town or somewhere?" the chief asked.

None of them did.

The chief knelt down to have a better look at the body. "Looks like he was stabbed right through the heart. At least the killer did us a favor leaving that knife for us. Maybe we can get some fingerprints off it. I take it none of you touched anything?"

"Only to roll him over on his back. We thought he might have been knocked out or drunk. That's when we saw he'd been killed and sent Fred to fetch you," Horace said. "Rolling him over seemed the right thing to do at the time. That's when we saw the knife."

"He wasn't killed with that knife," Beatrix said once again. "A palette knife wouldn't cut through butter, much less a cloth shirt, then puncture the skin to enter the chest cavity."

The chief ignored her, following his own agenda.

"Now, you sent your hired man into town to tell me. Why didn't you telephone right away?"

"There's no telephone line out here, and as you can see, no lights. Besides, even if we did have a telephone, Bobbie closes the switchboard at ten, so it wouldn't have done us any good," Harriet told him.

"Well, that stands to reason. Now, who actually found the body?"

"My wife, Clarice," Theo answered.

"I need to talk to her. Where is she?"

"On my father-in-law's boat, looking after my daughter, which is where I should be right now!" Harriet snapped. She folded her arms over her chest, staring defiantly at the chief.

"All in good time, Mrs. Walters. I'll let you go as soon as I've finished my investigation here," the chief said before turning to Theo, telling him that he would need to talk with Clarice. "It would have been better if she'd stayed out here,"

"I told them to stay on the boat," Horace said.

The chief knelt down on the grass to have a closer look at the body, pausing long enough to smell the man's breath. "No alcohol," he observed. He stood up. "I don't know what more we can do out here until daylight, other than to take the body into town. I want this area roped off until we have a look-see out here for evidence in the morning." He opened up his notebook again to make some notes. "Anyone else out here at the time?"

"You'll want to talk with John Reynolds, our caretaker. He was down at the beach with us for a campfire," Harriet said.

"And your name again?" He asked, looking at Beatrix

"Beatrix. Beatrix with an 'x' at the end, Beatrix Bronwyn Morgana Howell, Doctor Howell," she said slowly.

"That's quite the handle your parents saddled you with. Irish, is it?"

"Welsh," she answered firmly.

"It's still a mouthful. All right. You folks got a stretcher out here somewhere so we can take the body up to the building? I want a better look at the deceased before we take him into town," the chief asked. "I don't think we'll learn anything more, but I like to go by the book. Let's get him up there."

"I think there is one in the old carriage house out in back. John Reynolds would know where it is, but he's making sure everyone stays off the meadow," Harriet told him.

"All right, one of you go up to relieve this Reynolds fellow, and tell him to get the stretcher and bring it here. We'll need some help moving the body."

"Volunteering, sir," Fred offered, offering a half-salute, and then thinking better of it. The chief nodded his approval. While they waited Horace pulled out his pipe, filled it and lit it. To his surprise, Beatrix took it from him, enjoying a couple of deep puffs. "Nerves," she whispered.

They watched as John Reynolds returned with the stretcher, and he and the chief shifted the body onto the stretcher and carried it up to the Inn. "I'd like you two doctors to examine the body," the chief said when they put the stretcher on one of the tables in the dining hall.

"That's a job for the coroner," Horace objected. "And, there are three of us who are doctors," he reminded the chief.

"Yup. The coroner is our town doc, and he's gone to Pier Cove right now, tied up with Mrs. Johnson having a baby, so I can't get him until tomorrow morning, and this fellow isn't going anywhere on his own. I need a preliminary exam, so there you have it. You're it for right now." The chief answered firmly. "You want to bring up some lights so they can see better?" he asked John.

Harriet led Horace, Theo, and Beatrix out to the kitchen and found aprons for them. "Don't get too much blood on them or that old battle axe will fuss up a storm." The three of them rolled up their sleeves and washed up to their elbows.

"Just like the old days out in the country, isn't it, Theo?" Horace smiled as he explained to Beatrix, "Those were the days! Theo and I weren't even in medical school back then. Midnight calls out to a farm. Back then, Beatrix, Father would do operations on the dining room table. I was his assistant, and Theo, being the youngest, would administer the ether. Guess we won't need that tonight. I guess I shouldn't say it, but I sort of miss those days."

Horace beamed at the memory. "You want me to assist this time?" he asked. Theo shook his head and said, "Nah, you do it."

The three of them bent over the corpse. Horace, by default of his age and experience, instructed Garrison to take notes, while Theo and Beatrix assisted with the exam. Without proper instruments, they used table forks to spread open the shirt to expose the wound. "Very simply, instantaneous death by a sharp object through the heart. He was dead in seconds." Horace said as he straightened up. Beatrix saw him wince in pain, started to step closer to steady him, thought better of it and backed away.

"I concur," Theo added. "When your doctor does the autopsy he can give you a more formal report, but that's about the gist of it, wouldn't you say, Doctor Howell? Stabbed through the heart."

The chief grimaced in frustration. "Well, that's what we already knew. Whoever did this must have known what they were doing, or got lucky. You sure you can't tell me anything more than that?

"I'll remind you, again, it was not done with that knife," Beatrix said firmly.

"No, and how can you be so sure about that?" the chief asked.

Horace interrupted before she could answer. "Because she is a fully qualified pathologist, that's why. If she said he wasn't killed with that knife, then that's good enough for me. Carry on, Doctor Howell. Keep taking notes, chief, because you'll want to pay attention to what she has to say."

"Well, maybe he was carrying it and tripped and fell and stabbed himself," the chief suggested.

"That would be impossible. It is a palette knife. It is small, light, and very flexible. And dull. If Harriet will get one similar to this one I can demonstrate what I mean." She nodded in Harriet's direction to get one from the storage room. She waited for her to bring out a knife. Beatrix held it in one hand, flicking the blade with the index finger of her other hand. "As you can see, it is far too flimsy to inflict this sort of damage.

"Further, the victim was killed with a serrated knife, as you can see from the way the threads on the top of the shift have been ripped, not cleanly sliced or cut. There is no question in my mind about that. And, from the angle of the puncture wound, I believe the killer was at least a few inches taller than the victim, and right handed. No, I am very positive about that. Taller and right handed. It is very likely the assailant came up behind the victim by surprise, stabbed him in the chest, and then pulled the knife up when he pulled it out. And yes, probably a male. Very few women would be tall enough to do it, considering the height of the victim. An upward withdrawal."

Garrison looked at her, "Then what's the purpose of that little knife?"

"It may be a calling card. It is a tradition often used in a vendetta. It would not surprise me if the killer has killed before," Beatrix answered.

"A what?" the chief asked.

"A vendetta. It is Italian, more accurately Sicilian" a revenge killing for a real or alleged wrong or slight, or to remove an opponent and send a message."

Horace and Theo looked at each other. "Nitti" Horace said. "Or Capone," Theo answered.

"I believe that would be mere and unwarranted speculation at this time, doctors, and potentially counterproductive in a criminal investigation," Beatrix told them.

The chief turned toward Harriet. "So, you just let anyone waltz through here willy-nilly?"

Beatrix quickly answered. "I doubt they waltz. Why would someone waltz at an art school?"

The chief glared at her and rolled his eyes, returning his attention to Harriet. "So, let's try this again. Our John Doe comes out here to Ox-Bow, just walks in like he belongs here, gets himself killed, and no one knows his name, where he's from, who he's with or been with, or anything else. We don't have a murder weapon, and whoever did it put that little do-hickey thing in his chest to throw us off the trail. That's rich! That's really rich, isn't it? We don't know anything useful at all. All we know is that we've got a dead man. Well, I can have this wrapped up in time for breakfast!"

"Despite your penchant for sarcasm, I believe it will take longer than that," Beatrix said. The chief rewarded her with a fierce glare.

"All right, we're getting nowhere fast tonight. That's about all we can do out here. I am giving you permission to go home. You're all staying on the *Aurora*, I take it? Well, go home and stay there. You don't take a step off the boat without my say-so, you hear? I'll be interviewing all of you again tomorrow, is that clear?

"Mrs. Walters, see if you can find a sheet or blanket or something to cover him up. You got a truck out here so we can get his body into town?"

She said that she and John would find something.

Garrison turned to the rest of them. "Like I said: Go back to the boat and stay there. And I want your caretaker posted on the road. No one comes in or goes out tonight. Police orders, understood?"

"That's going to make a long night for John," Harriet objected. "He's worked all day; you can't expect him to stay up all night."

"Too bad," the chief shrugged. "I want him on duty."

Horace, Theo, and Beatrix went back to the kitchen to take off their aprons and wash up. Horace was about to leave when Fred knocked on the back door. "Someone to see you, boss."

"All right," he said quietly. To his surprise, it was Paulette. Even more surprising, she was sober and quiet. "I heard what happened. Johnny told me. It's awful, someone getting killed out here like that" she whispered. She pulled up the hem of her skirt to get her flask and took a quick nip. "Have some. It'll help you sleep tonight," she said as she handed it to him. "Keep it, in case you need it. I got plenty more where that came from."

Horace looked around and put the flask into his pocket. No one had spied them.

"Beatrix, I think under these circumstances you should stay onboard tonight with the rest of us," Horace said. "We still have a spare cabin or two."

"Thank you. I am perfectly comfortable where I am."

"I understand that, but right now there's a murderer on the loose, and you've been in on this most of the night. I don't think you are safe out here, and you will be much safer on the boat. I'd like you to think about joining us."

She stared away from him as she considered what he'd said. Quietly, she answered, "Perhaps it would be safer. Thank you."

Mrs. Garwood was waiting for them on the gangplank. "Harriet, now, don't you worry. Everything is just fine. Clarice and I got

Phoebe to bed and she fell asleep right away. Clarice is sitting with her now in case she wakes. She smiled as Harriet hurried down the hallway to her daughter's cabin, eager to look in on her.

"And Beatrix, Mrs. Garwood will show you to your cabin. The Minnesota is made up, isn't it? You'll be all right there," Horace said. "As for the rest of us, let's get some sleep. We're in for a long day come morning."

The local physician needed very little encouragement to invite the Balfour Brothers and what Chief Garrison described as, "that woman doctor," to attend the autopsy. Howard Landis a congenial man who was, a few years out of medical school at Northwestern University and an internship at Stanford, warmly welcomed the three of them to what he called his "cottage hospital". As they were scrubbing up he apologized for the small size of the facility, adding, "I'll bet you three never had something this, well, rustic."

Theo laughed. "Reminds me of when my brother and I were starting out. Sort of makes me feel right at home."

Dr. Landis smiled in gratitude. "Mainly, it's bread and butter work. Broken bones, abrasions, beans up the nose or in the ear, babies, that sort of thing. Sniffles and gout. Nothing too exciting or dangerous. Anything we can't handle we send up to Holland or Grand Rapids."

He chuckled when Beatrix said she worked with Dr. Lester Sacket in his laboratories at the university: "I heard he's a real bearcat to work with. Well, let's get started."

For the next hour the four of them were bent over an examination table, taking turns exploring the naked, but carefully draped body. When he finally straightened up, Doctor Landis said, "You were certainly thorough last night, especially since you were working in the dark. I had some professors talk about how their fathers did it like that in the pioneer days. It won't surprise you we were both working by lantern last night. The family I was attending doesn't have the electric yet, either.

"And, I'm sure you are right about the serrated blade, maybe six to eight inches long. We could examine the heart a bit more closely, but I don't think it would show us anything we don't already know. In layman's terms, a knife through the heart, and that's all they wrote. I suspect it was too dark for you to notice the knick on a rib," he said with a slight smile, delighted in scoring a point with the Balfour Brothers.

"Yes, yes it was," Theo told him.

"So, Chief, that's about all we can tell you. It's up to you to figure out who he is and why someone wanted to kill him," Doctor Landis said. "That, and figuring out who did it."

"I believe there is a good chance he's Italian," Beatrix said quietly.

"How do you figure that?" Theo asked.

She flashed a rare smile. "I cheated. I looked at the tags on his shirt and jacket." She nodded at the pile of clothing folded up on a table. "Both say 'Milano' – Milan, Italy. He could have bought them on his travels, of course, but his underthings were also made in Italy. Again, Milan, according to the tags. A man might buy his outer garments on his holidays, but rarely his personal garments.

"His shoes are also from Milan." She held up one of his shoes so the others could see the stamp under the leather tongue. "And the shoes tell us much more about his life, and the events leading up to last night. If you look carefully, you will see some very faint grass stains on the toes, probably from walking across the meadow, and yet, I am certain he lived in a city. You can see where the soles are evenly worn, except under the ball of his feet, but no gouges or scratches to indicate he spent much time walking on gravel or rough terrain. He walked on sidewalks and inside."

The chief was about to say something, but Beatrix held up a hand to stop him and continued. "The soles are worn far more than the heals. Again, you can see this spot under the ball of the foot. That means he was primarily in a house or office much of the time, likely with smooth floors. But most importantly, he wasn't dragged to the place where we found him."

The Balfour Brothers and Doctor Landis stared at her in awe. "What about being carried there?" Horace asked. "That meadow is dark, and all of us were down at the bonfire. We wouldn't have seen a thing after dark?"

"That is very unlikely. Look again at the torso and his shirt. The blood flowed down the front left side of his chest and abdomen, then trickled off the left side of his body as it coagulated. More importantly, there is relatively little blood for a wound this size, which confirms almost instantaneous death. If he had been carried, he would have been face down over the killer's shoulders, the weight of his body would have forced more blood out of the wound, and the shirt would have a much wider blood splotch. The killer would also have had blood on his clothing, which, if he was an assassin, he would have avoided that at all costs."

"How do you know that?" the chief demanded.

"The palette knife. The killer was probably experienced, if not a professional assassin," she answered.

"That's the vendetta thing you were going on about last night?" he asked.

"In part. But if the victim had been killed somewhere and carried, he would have been dropped on his back, then the knife put in the wound and rolled the body over. That would not be likely because it would have taken time to get out the palette knife, find the wound, and insert it. Even if the killer had time on his hands, it would have been a risk he would not have wanted to take. Therefore, I believe he was killed on the spot."

The men stared at her in silence, stunned by how much information she had told them.

Chief Garrison grimaced, "Now, if you could just tell us the victim's name....."

"No identification on him?" Horace asked.

"Nothing. His pockets were picked clean. And you are certain you didn't find anything on him; you know, found it and put it in your pocket by accident.? So, despite everything you just told us, it still looks to me like it was a stick-up job gone bad," the chief replied, pulling the sheet up over the body.

"I think we ought to leave a little work for you, Chief, finding the victim's name and chasing down the killer. We've done our part," Doctor Landis said. He turned to the Balfours and Beatrix. "I'll write up the report, and then I'd like you to sign off on it."

"Tell you what; you get it written and bring it over to my boat later this afternoon, and join us for dinner. Sound jake to you?" Horace asked.

The young physician smiled. "Jake. I'd be honoured. And, I know I'll learn plenty from you, Doctor Howell. Hope to see you there. We can have a right lively discussion over dinner. Say, you're not having fish are you? I've had it five nights running, and one more night of it and I'll sprout fins."

Doctor Horace winced. "I can assure you that Mrs. Garwood wouldn't dream of cooking it. All right, I'm ready to go. You coming back with us, Beatrix?"

"No, not yet."

"Library," Horace said to Theo when they returned to the boat. "We need to work out a plan."

"My plan right now is for some sleep. I'm half-dead I'm so tired. I don't know about you, but I'm not some young resident who can go without sleep. I didn't sleep very well last night, between that murder and Clarice jumping every time she heard something."

"Me too," Horace said. "Look, this won't take long. The way I see it, the best thing we can do is get Harriet and Beatrix to move onto the boat until we know what's happening. Maybe being out at Ox-Bow is safe for Harriet during the day; I don't know about her being on her own at night, and we don't want Phoebe in danger, either. They should both stay here. And that cottage where Beatrix is camped out is too isolated. They'd both be safer here."

Theo let out another long yawn. "You think the killer is still around here? That's a bit of a stretch, isn't it? You'd think if you just killed someone in cold blood you'd want to disappear fast." He looked at Horace's withering glare and retracted his comment. "A bit too obvious, isn't it? Better to stick around and look normal. Yeah, I see your point, especially if it is someone from around here."

Horace smiled. "And I say we turn Fred loose to do a bit of snooping."

"He'll like that. Right down his alley," Theo agreed. "Look, there is something bothering me, and we have to face it. It's Beatrix. We all saw her get up and wander off when we had that campfire. She was gone for a long time...."

Horace waved him off. "Maybe she just went behind the bushes to visit Mrs. Murphy."

"I thought of that too, but she never said anything to Garrison about it last evening, and didn't mention it this morning, either. I know what you're going to say: Garrison never asked. And maybe she would have been uncomfortable mentioning something, well, personal. But just the same, she seemed to know an awful lot about how that fellow was murdered, even where he came from."

Horace disagreed. "Theo, she's a pathologist, and if she works with Doctor Sackett, she's one of the best in the country. She's trained to see everything and draw conclusions. I don't think there's anything more to it than that."

"Yeah? I'm not so sure. I have a feeling she knows a lot more than she's letting on. Look, I'm not as trusting as you are, that's all, especially when it comes to someone we hardly know. That is, unless you know more about her than you're letting on," Theo said. He didn't want to provoke Horace, but quickly made up his mind to keep a closer eye on her as he changed the subject. "Anyway, how come you're so full of energy? I'm half loopy from lack of sleep. You're mind's clicking like a locomotive doing ninety. What's going on?"

"Just feeling better. Like my old self again," Horace flashed a smile that raised Theo's anxiety. "Must be having something exciting to do for a change instead of sitting in a rocking chair."

It was only after his brother left the study that Horace realized he was once again drained to the point of exhaustion. He went down to his cabin, locked the door behind him, and stretched out on his bed. He awakened a few hours later to the sound of a piano being played very badly and raised voices. It took him a half minute to remember that he had bought the piano for Phoebe. "And that's why I avoid music. Thunderation!" he growled as he suffered through the racket before getting up.

He found Phoebe and Roletta sitting on the piano bench with Lloyd Stoddard leaning over their shoulders, trying to squeeze past her to play. "Look. Just listen for a moment. This isn't sacrilege. It's classical music! It is plain old fashioned theme and variation. It's what you long-hairs do all the time. Just let me show you what I mean. Play something by that Chopin fellow you're always going on about."

"I will not tarnish the memory of the world's greatest composer just so you can mock him!" she retorted.

"Fine! Then play something by someone else, woman. Just let me show you what I mean, that's all I'm asking. Play "Twinkle, twinkle, little star" for all I care."

Roletta let out a long dramatic sigh and snapped, "Fine!" and began playing the old gospel hymn "What a Friend We Have in Jesus" as if it were meant to be a funeral dirge. After she went through the chorus and refrain Stoddard stopped her. "So, are we agreed that's the theme? Good! Now, let's do what the classical composers did and start the variations. Give me a little room to sit down, would you, Little Sister?" he asked Phoebe. She gave him her place on the bench, and he played the song once more, making it into a quasi Bach fugue, then slipping into a march style. "First theme; then variations. Same music." He converted it into a waltz, then a polka. "And now, we move into the modern age," and he launched into a ragtime version. "See what I mean? All the same tune, just in different forms. That wasn't so bad, now was it"?"

Roletta was defeated and she knew it. Her mouth opened and shut, and then she exploded in anger. "Be that as it may! I will not have you teaching this impressionable young girl such shameless noise. Noise! The way you play it isn't even proper music. And it certainly was not the pure way the composer wrote it!" She stood up and stalked toward the door, pausing just enough to shake a finger in Doctor Horace's face. "And, and, and, this is all your fault. I will never set foot on this boat again as long as that odious little man is here!"

"Promise?" Horace asked.

She glared. "For two dollars I'd part his hair with my meat cleaver, and don't think I don't mean it!" She stormed down the gangplank.

"Thunderation! What in the name of Louis Pasteur and Madame Currie is going on around here?" Horace demanded.

"Ah, that old battleship thinks she's the only one who can play the piano. It has to be done her way or not at all. I was just trying to expand her musical education a little and bring her into the modern age. She got a bit hot under the collar about it, that's all," Stoddard said.

"What's this talk about taking a meat cleaver to someone? I could hear a woman shouting half way down the street," the police chief said as he came up the gangplank. "Sounds to me like something I ought to know about, seeing as how we just had a murder." He wasn't smiling or laughing.

"Oh, just Mrs. Hansen blowing off a little steam. Seems she doesn't care much for any music but the stuff written by a bunch of dead long-hairs," Stoddard explained.

"I'm with you on that one," Garrison smiled. "That sort of stuff either puts me to sleep or grates on my nerves. I guess it's okay for those who like it, but I'd rather hear something a little more up-to-date. Now, that's not what I'm here for. I heard some hollering about a meat cleaver. Tell me about that."

"Hot air hooey, that's all," Horace said. "Just Mrs. Hansen...."

The chief cut him off. "Oh, her. I know who you mean. Well, I still want to talk to her. Piano teacher, you say?"

"That, and she's the summer cook at Ox-Bow," Horace told him.

"Cook! You don't say? That means she knows how to use a knife, doesn't it? Well, I'm adding her to my list of suspects right along with the rest of you."

"Am I a suspect, too?" Phoebe gasped. The chief just looked at her and shook his head before he went to find Mrs Hansen.

"I don't think so, Phoebs," her grandfather said.

The girl's lower lip jutted out as she winked, "I never get to have any fun."

Horace trailed behind the chief out to the deck, leaning on the rail as he watched him quickly walk down the street in pursuit of Mrs. Hansen. He continued watching as Fred parked the car alongside the boat and Harriet hurried up to the deck.

"Oh, good. You're here. Look, I hope I've done the right thing without asking you first," Harriet told Horace as soon as she came up to him.

"Seems to me like it's about your turn. I've been doing it enough. Go on."

"It's this. Doctor Landis brought Beatrix out to the school, and as it happened our caretaker, you remember John, said he'd walk with her up to Doctor Mason's cabin, just to be sure everything was all right. Well, the long and short of it is, it wasn't! Someone had obviously tried jimmying open the door. When she told me, I convinced her that she would be better off staying in town. The only problem is, there isn't a room available anywhere, and she said she'd go on home. Horace, she already packed her bag.

"So, you offered to let her stay in a cabin here, right? Good thinking. Of course, she's welcome. I was just thinking the same thing. And, you might as well know, it would be better if you moved in too, at least for a little while. You can bunk in with Phoebe, or the room next to her, whichever you want or think best."

Harriet momentarily ignored the invitation. "Could you come down and speak with her? I think it would be better if the invitation came from you."

It took some solid convincing to get Beatrix to move onto the *Aurora* and to assure her that she would not be a burden for Mrs. Garwood, nor be in the way. "It would be safer here, especially at night, at least for the short-term," he told her.

"I understand, but I'm accustomed to flying solo," she said flatly, her eyes down.

"I appreciate that more than you might realize," Horace said. She took up at him and understood what he meant, giving a very wan smile. "All things considered, with a murderer on the loose and maybe in the area, and now someone trying to break into your cabin, this will be safer."

"Perhaps it's just some of the mischief," she suggested.

"You are probably right. But until we know....." Horace told her, convinced it was more than a mere prank. It was a direct message. He didn't want to debate the point any further, "Fred, would you take Beatrix's grip up to her cabin. She's in the Minnesota."

Mrs. Garwood came out on the deck to greet her, taking Beatrix' suitcase from Fred's hand. "I'll take you down to your cabin, and then you've got about an hour before dinner. We ring the first gong a quarter-hour before we sit down, and then again ten minutes later."

"A gong?" she asked.

"Yes. Just be thankful we're tied up in town. When we're on the water, the boss sometimes let's Fred fire the cannon to announce dinner. Scares me half to death. Be grateful for small mercies, as my Ma used to say."

Horace summoned Theo, Fred, and Captain Garwood into the library. Despite their curiosity, no one asked anything about the heavy box the captain carried in with him.

"So, here we go again," Fred smiled with pure delight.

"Here we go again," the captain echoed. "That's why I brought...."

Horace interrupted. "We'll come to that in a moment. Now, we all know what's happened out to Ox-Bow, but what we don't know is if we're in any danger or not, but I don't think we should take chances. We were all out at the camp when the man was killed, so let's make some plans because it just could mean we're all targets."

"What's this idea about bringing Beatrix on board?" Theo asked quietly. "I'm not sure that was a good idea."

"I do," Horace shot back. He and Theo often disagreed, but only in private. In front of others, they made a united front. This time was different.

"Look, I know the four of us grew up together. Say what you want about going to the same school, the same church, even the same profession, or anything else. But will you keep in mind we haven't seen her in years, almost fifty of them, in fact. We don't know anything about her except what's she told us, and let's face it, it isn't much. She might not even be straight with us. She might be a crackerjack pathologist AND a crackpot murderer, for all we know. We're taking a big risk. You're taking a big risk with your granddaughter here, too."

"That will do!" Horace's voice rose in anger. "If you are right, then we've got her right where we can keep an eye on her. Meanwhile, our job is ..."

Fred interrupted with a compromise. "Then what we need is someone to stay on sentry duty, especially at night. Keep watch to make sure the enemy doesn't surprise us with a raid."

"Oddly enough, that almost sounds sensible," Theo sighed.

"We ought to put trip lines on the gangplank so they can't slip through the perimeter. And, train those search lights on the ropes!" Fred suggested.

"Ah, why don't we just raise the gangplank at night? And, we've already got lights on the sides of the boat?" the captain suggested. He winced, "Both sides – by land or by sea."

"Well, that'll work. But we need to pass out the rifles and fix bayonets!" Fred countered. "We could send a couple of scout out on shore to keep watch, and if they try anything funny, get a jump on them. My old lieutenant said we had to keep the Hun surrounded. He was right, too. Can't let your guard down. Not for a second!"

"Oh good! Just what we need. A bunch of trigger-happy old-timers shooting at each other in the dark," Theo snapped. "No!"

"Doctor Theo is right," the captain said. He opened the box. "These are fish bats," he said as he held up what looked like a short thick billy club. "Fishermen use them if they get a northern pike on their line." He lightly whacked the bat into his open palm. "Like that, only a lot harder. I got one for each cabin and a few spares. One for the galley, another one for you here in your office if you're up late, boss, and one for each head."

"Good thinking, Captain. If there's a gang of cutthroats we can slip up on them and take them out one at a time without the others being any the wiser!" Fred chortled in delight.

"Thank you, Captain. Good thinking. Now gentlemen, let's get back to business. Fred, I want you to do a bit of snooping around town. Just keep your eyes and ears open. Go have coffee, talk with people, just do what you do best. And make sure you leave the car keys in the galley. That way, when you're off on a reconnaissance mission, if we need transportation, we'll have the keys."

Fred jumped to his feat and saluted. "Yes, Sir!" Captain Garwood shot him a look that returned him to his seat.

"Theo, I think it would be better if you handle Garrison and Landis. You're better at dealing with people than, ah, well, anyone else. People seem to like you," Horace told his brother.

"You're right about that," Theo grimaced, knowing that Horace was talking about himself. "I'll see what I can do, but I doubt we'll get anything out of Garrison as long as he has us on his list of suspects. Landis might be a lot more helpful, seeing as how we're visiting firemen. Horace, are we trying to catch the killer or something?"

"No. Not at all. That's the chief's job. All I want to do is keep us all safe. That's it. Period. But we need any information we can get to stay safe. Like I've been saying, last summer we blundered ourselves right into an ambush and got out of it by just pure dumb luck. We don't want that to happen again. No, let's face it, we're too old to playing detective. Now, does everyone understand that? We're just looking after our own safety? Is that clear?"

There was a soft knock at the door, and Harriet opened it a crack. "Oh, sorry. I'm interrupting," she apologized.

"Not at all," Theo said. "Gentlemen, shall we?" He stood up to lead the others out the door.

"And this is for you, Mrs. Walters," the captain said, handing her a bat. She looked at him. "The boss will explain."

CHAPTER SEVEN

"Do I want to know about this?" Harriet asked, holding up the wooden bat. "Or, should I have a dose of your prescription medicine in your hidden cabinet first?" she asked brightly.

"Better take your medicine first and then I'll explain," Horace said.

"I thought so." She watched as he lifted out the bottle. "By the way, with Nitti out of the picture, who's your new supplier?"

"Fred doesn't exactly share that information. One or two fingers?" Horace asked. Harriet held up three.

"Now, about the bats," Horace explained. "For the time being, we're buttoning things up a bit more tightly around here. Nothing to be worried about, but we're being a little more cautious until things settled down."

"That explains why Fred looks so happy. Let me guess, you sent him out on reconnaissance And, I already know how to use one of these. Every mother teaches her daughter that a rolling pin isn't just for pie crusts and cookies. It's a secret we pass down from generation to generation, and you'll be happy to know I've already taught Phoebe. My mother gave it to me when I was engaged to your son. So, here's to a summer of surprises, and may they all come to a quick end!" she said, holding up her glass to toast him. She took a sip and winced. "That almost makes me miss Nitti."

"You don't look like having a drink was the only thing on your mind. Right?"

Harriet looked down at her lap for a long time before barely whispering, "I've decided to write a letter of resignation. This summer has been a disaster. I've failed Mr. Fursman and the rest of them. They threw me right into the deep end of the pool, and I don't think it's because they thought I could do it. They just needed someone, and I've failed. Phoebe, all of you, the students, the teachers. I can't control the vandalism, and now this murder. It's been a war of attrition, and I'm losing. I can't take anymore of it."

Horace said nothing, giving her time to continue.

She looked at him, her eyes wet with tears. "I'm a teacher, not an administrator. I never even wanted to be a teacher but Mother convinced me I should be one in case I ever had to be on my own."

"Which you have been. I know. I understand."

"I've told Phoebe the same thing. Teaching is one thing, but not this job. I'm failing at it. Do you have any idea how I spend my days. I don't teach. I shuffle papers. Papers, papers, and more papers. I hate inventory, and that's all this is – an inventory of paper. And the murder was the last straw. I quit!"

"You write your letter yet?" Horace asked slowly.

"No. I wanted to tell you first."

"I truly appreciate that. But, I don't think you really want to resign, do you? If you did, you would have written the letter and then told me," Horace said softly. "You might not be an administrator, but you are definitely not a quitter." He gave her time to let his words sink in.

"I know, but I can't see anything else I can do. I don't want to wait to be fired."

Horace thought it over before slowly saying. "I know, and the truth is, I've seen this before. Plenty of times. I've had young resident surgeons who did a routine operation, bread and butter work, and did it by the book, and suddenly their patient died. They were sure they failed and weren't cut out to be a doctor. They would have quit, too. They came into my office or talked it over with Theo, sometimes with a resignation in hand. And you know what I did? I tore up their letter and told them to get back to work. I even had a gardener who accidently broke a rake and thought I should fire him."

"Isn't that what you're telling me to do? Not quit?

"Harriet, I learned a long time ago never to tell you what you should do. I'm just asking you think about it first.

"But I can't do it on my own. If you could figure out who was murdered and who did it, then maybe things would be different."

"What makes you think you're on your own? And, as for figuring out who killed that fellow, we're already working on it." It was a fib, a big one, but it made Harriet feel better, and Horace couldn't think of anything better to say. She finished her drink and said she would think it over.

Doctor Landis arrived half-an-hour before dinner, and Horace led him, Theo, and Beatrix into the library so they could look at the autopsy papers. "Footnotes?" Theo asked, thinking it was over-reaching.

"I know it's a bit irregular, but I explained the medical terms for laymen. I thought it might be helpful to the chief and, if he gets lucky, the county prosecutor," Landis explained.

"If the notes are at the conclusion of the document they are end-notes, not footnotes," Beatrix said.

"Well, yes, of course. Endnotes," Landis corrected himself.

They passed the pages from one to another, and after they were finished reading Horace said, "Well, I think you've got just about everything covered. Any ideas about the knife or instrument used to kill him."

"Nothing that Doctor Howell hasn't already told us. It was definitely serrated. I verified that with a much closer examination of the body and his shirt. Probably it was serrated on both edges of the blade."

"I disagree with that," Beatrix said. The fabric is cut on only one side. It is sliced at the bottom where the point entered, but ripped on the top. Therefore, it could only have been serrated on one side. Assuming it was a standard knife and not another instrument, the serrations would be on the bottom, and that tells us the killer held it upside down. If it was an amateur, then they got lucky; if it was a professional, then it stands to reason."

Doctor Landis all but ignored her. "And since the four of us were present at the autopsy, we should all sign it. I propose we initial each page and put our signatures on the final page. All agreed?" He was reaching for the pen in his shirt pocket, and suddenly froze. "What was that? A fire alarm?" he asked.

"It's the first gong to announce dinner. We'll have to see whether or not it is one of Mrs. Garwood's burnt offerings," Horace teased.

Just as soon as she had rushed through dinner Phoebe asked to be excused from the table so she could practice her piano. And, it wasn't long after that before Captain and Mrs. Garwood quickly, and very noisily, began clearing the table and carrying the dishes to the kitchen. "That racket is pretty rough on the ears, if you don't mind me saying so, Boss," the Captain whispered. Royce nodded in agreement, soon leaving for the relative quiet of his cabin off the engine room. Horace watched him enviously as he made his escape.

Even Clarice winced repeatedly at each sour note, and then suggested they should all go into town for some ice cream at Parissh's drugstore. When Theo didn't seem eager to stir out of his chair she pulled him to his feet. Fred also took that as his cue to slip away, saying, "Think I'll go and reconnoitre somewhere." Under his breath he added, "somewhere without that racket." Finally Harriet realized she already had suffered enough, and went into the library to tell Phoebe to close the piano because they were going for ice cream.

Horace breathed a sigh of relief. When he glanced over at Beatrix, he saw she was motionless, staring straight ahead, hiding out in some world of her own.

"Grandfather, don't you want to come with us? You like ice cream!" she asked. He waved her off and said he was going to stay right where he was, adding that he had had enough for one day. The girl was disappointed, but quickly tried again, "Doctor Howell, would you like to come with us? It's my treat if Grandfather will give me some money?" Beatrix gravely thanked her, but also declined.

It was only when the group had walked down Water Street and turned left at the white House that Horace breathed a sigh of relief. "Blessed silence. I've done some boneheaded things in my life, but I swear, that piano tops them all."

"She may improve in time," Beatrix said.

"I doubt any of us will live that long."

They sat in awkward silence, looking at the pedestrians and traffic until Beatrix quietly apologized, "I don't do what people call small talk very well."

"That's good. Neither do I. I prefer silence unless there is something important to say. That's part of the problem with the world today. It's too noisy, and people talk too much. I was in a shop the other day and the owner had a radio blaring away to entertain us. That's what he said – to entertain. I don't need to be entertained every moment. No one does."

"You've always been that way, haven't you?" she asked. "Feeling like the outsider always looking in, and never feeling like you really belong on the inside. I do."

Horace thought over her question before admitting, "Yes, I think so. Work, study, books have always been easier. Safer. Now, Theo can walk into a room and everyone's his friend. I walk in and I feel like I'm invisible."

Beatrix laughed. "I walk into a room and people reach for their coats as if a blizzard blew in." She was quiet again, and then uncharacteristically chuckled and asked, "Horace, do you remember the game we made up back in Sunday school? The one where people thought we could read each other's mind. Remember it?"

"No. Growing up was too long ago," he said. "Besides, I'd rather not remember that time."

She was undeterred. "We had it all worked out. If you wanted me to say 'yes' to something, or I did to you, we'd always as a question with a positive. Remember how we did it? Do you want to? Would you like to?" Should we? And if we wanted a 'no' answer we'd ask it with a negative. You don't want to? You don't need to? Oh, you must remember!"

It was his turn to laugh. "Now that you mention it, yes I do. That's a long time ago. The more we did it, the more we could add to it. We had our mothers and teachers flummoxed. We should try it sometime on Theo and Clarice. I wonder if they remember us doing it?"

His question was met with more silence until Clarice changed the subject. "I saw a box of cigars on your desk."

"I prefer a pipe, but people give me cigars, and then I end up giving them away." He did not realize it was a question, not an observation.

"Well, if you're giving one away now, I won't say 'no'."

She watched as he got up and stiffly made his way into his study, returning with two cigars and the lighter Fred had given him.

"That's unique," she said.

"Fred got it up in Holland the other day. It seems that some old war buddy takes old grenades and makes them into lighters." Horace handed it to her. "Don't pull out the pin or it won't light. Just squeeze the handle twice and the flame comes out the top. He watched her light her cigar as he filled his pipe. "You'd be surprised what he finds. My guess is there's more stuff on the boat he's squirreled away than I know about. He makes life interesting." He lit his pipe. "I envy him somehow. He has fun."

She took a long pull on her cigar and slowly blew out three smoke rings. "Good cigar. So, tell me Horace, are we really in some sort of danger?"

"What makes you ask that?"

She flashed a thin smile. "First, you turned down going out for some ice cream. Phoebe tells me you like it, and I know you love her so you had to have a good reason not to go. Probably, you are keeping watch in case someone tries to slip aboard. That's why we're sitting on this side, instead of looking at the water and the other boats, and away from the noise. And then, Captain Garwood was passing out truncheons, and they're either meant to be thrown at a rat or for repelling boarders. I don't think there are any rats, so it must be the latter. After dinner Fred said he was going out to scout around town. I also noticed when you came out of your study the right side of your jacket is weighted down by something, and the flap is tucked in on your pocket. The left flap is out, which means you put something into your pocket, and that leads me to suspect you're carrying a small pistol. So, I'll ask again, do you really think we're in some sort of danger?"

"That obvious?"

"That obvious."

"You don't miss much, do you? I don't know, really. I just think we ought to be a bit more careful until we know how things spell out."

"It could be nothing more than a robbery that ended with a murder. The victim didn't have any money on him," Beatrix reminded him.

"That's the point. He didn't have anything on him. His pockets were picked clean. I have a strange feeling, that's all. So does Theo. So, until then...."

"Until then, we enjoy the evening," she told him.

They sat in silence, Horace enjoying his pipe, and Beatrix her cigar. Some of the older couples on the sidewalks were beginning to return to their guest rooms, leaving only the younger people, some of them not too steady on their feet, walking to the Big Pavilion. Beatrix finished her cigar and flicked the last two inches into the water. "It's bitter. Good night, Doctor Horace Balfour," she said flatly.

Horace remained on deck, keeping a casual watch while he waited another half hour before his party came up the gangplank, with Fred trailing behind. "All present and accounted for, Sir! I spotted them on the street and trailed them until the last half block." He snapped a salute to his boss. "Unless you think I ought to be on sentry duty tonight, I thought I might get a bit of shut-eye?" he suggested. Horace nodded toward the cabins.

"And time for you to get some sleep, too, young lady," Harriet told her daughter.

"I have to give Grandfather a hug goodnight, first," she yawned. "Grandfather, the ice cream doesn't taste nearly as good when you aren't along." He watched as the two women also went to their cabins.

"Anything?" Theo asked his brother after the others were gone.

"Nothing. All quiet."

"I'll bet you had a raucous time with Beatrix. Did she even speak? Why don't you get some rest. I'll stay up for a while," Theo said. He and Horace watched Gar work the little electric motor raise the gangplank.

"If you're staying up, you'd better take this," Horace said as he offered his pistol.

Theo chuckled, patting his jacket pocket. "I've got my own. Clarice gave it to me at the end of the summer. Would you believe it's the one she took off Frank Nitti? I doubt he misses it. Say, Fred told me he saw some tough looking characters over to the pool hall. I suppose he'll sniff around there tomorrow and find something."

"I'll stay up with you for a while," Horace offered.

"I'm a big boy now; I don't need an older brother looking after me. Leastwise, not all the time. Get some rest."

Horace retreated to his cabin for what became a sleepless night. Every sound, even the most routine ones that he would have slept through on most nights, kept him awake. Even when he did drift off for a few moments, he was plagued by memories of the past. It was Beatrix's fault, dredging up memories that he had buried and wanted left far in the past.

He was not the only one who found sleep elusive. Theo sat up late on a deck chair, supposedly to keep watch for another hour or so, watching the street to see if anyone took an unusual interest in the boat. There was more to it than that. It was Beatrix. To be sure, she had an unusual personality, drifting in and out of conversations, sometimes her abruptness when she spoke and rarely making eye contact. That wasn't nearly as bad as how she made such pinpoint observations and then deductions.

She seemed to somehow know more than anyone else, and long before Garrison or even his brother could come to the same conclusion. It was almost as if she was leading them on, playing a game with them, perhaps even daring them somehow, or leading them down blind alleys. That stuff about the victim being Italian, just from looking at the tags on his clothing. Fine. Maybe he was. Or, maybe she already knew him and knew he was Italian.

Theo got up and paced around the deck, trying to convince himself he was checking to make sure all was safe, while he tried to understand Beatrix. He couldn't figure her out. And, what truly worried and frightened him was how Horace was constantly defending her, refusing to consider her as a possible suspect. She was up to something – he was sure of it.

He walked slowly around the deck, and by the third lap convinced himself that Beatrix was leading Horace into a lethal trap. Just what sort of a trap, and the reason for it challenged him.

Even when he finally went down to his cabin, his mind was still whirling away. Clarice was breathing steadily, sound asleep. Theo quietly undressed and slipped into his nightclothes, putting the pistol on the floor next to the bed. If anything was going to happen during the wee hours, he would be prepared.

CHAPTER EIGHT

After finding it impossible to go to sleep, Horace finally drifted off a few hours before daybreak, then slept much later than usual. The *Aurora* was unusually quiet, and he found Theo sitting alone at a table, a bit bleary-eyed, reading. "Everyone gone, Theo?" he asked.

"Almost. Fred drove Harriet and Beatrix out to the school in the car and came back a while ago. Don't worry, your keys are in the galley. Apparently, some of the local painters decided to go out there to continue painting, something of a show of the flag that they won't be scared off. If you ask me, they want to meet a new artist by the name of Hoerman. Carl Hoerman, I think Harriet said. Clarice is having a coffee morning with some women from Evanston who summer here and raise money for the Episcopal Church. My guess is that a coffee morning means it extends to lunch and probably bridge after that. Royce asked Gar if he could go fishing, so he's off somewhere. And, the Garwoods are probably staying on board since Madame Chopin is coming over to give Phoebe a long piano lesson this afternoon. I don't know about you, but I want to get out of here before she comes."

Horace smiled. "I'm with you! I don't need another row like yesterday. I was hoping Fred would be out doing a little scouting around town."

"That brings up something I want to discuss with you. Now, I distinctly remember you saying we were not going to get involved in a murder investigation, that it was Garrison's job, not ours. And then, lo and behold this morning Harriet thanked me for helping to solve the crime." Theo's voice was firm. "I take it there is a change in plans I don't know about."

"Well, that's about the size of it. A change in plans; you're absolutely right. Thunderation! She came into my study last evening and told me she was going to resign. She didn't say it, but she's scared. And, well, I just couldn't....." his voice trailed off.

"You just couldn't resist helping a damsel in distress. I know."

"It's not like that. I couldn't say 'no' to her. It's Harriet and Phoebe. Family. We just can't walk away from them like that."

"I know, and you're probably right. I'm not surprised. Nor am I surprised you'd change plans without telling me. Well, it does surprise me to think of you having a heart. Soon as you're ready let's go out there and have another look around."

"Theo, I do have a heart. It's just that I don't wear it on my sleeve. I have a heart. Let's go."

The two brothers were just about to drive away when the police chief pulled up behind them. "Glad I caught up with you. I've got some news. We provisionally identified the deceased. Apparently, he had a room at one of the guest houses just off Park Street and didn't return home the other night. The owner called me, wondering if I had him in the lock-up or knew something, so I went by their place with a picture of him laid out on the slab. Not the best picture, pretty gruesome now that I think about it, but they knew him. He's a fellow by the name of Flavio Pulchini," Garrison said in triumph.

"Provisionally identified? What does that mean? He is or he isn't?" Horace asked.

"I'll get to that in the by and by. But get this. He's an Italian painter, and he must have been a good one because he taught at some academy over in Florence, the one in Italy. From what I can figure out, he must have come over here this summer to look around the art museums in the big cities and worked his way west to Chicago, and then decided to come up this way. We don't know why he did it, but it must have been to have a look at Ox-Bow and see what it's like. Maybe he was figuring on taking some ideas back home.

"Anyways, I sent a telegram down to the art museum to let them know we'd found him dead, and I got one right back saying they'd gotten hold of the Italian consulate in Chicago. I didn't know they had one of them there. Anyways, they decided that since this victim's an important man, they had to stick their noses into it. They're sending their top man and a couple of his helpers up here on the train. Probably they think they can run the investigation or something, but that's not going to happen. I'm running things here whether they like it or not."

"You said you'd provisionally identified him," Horace said.

"Well, they're bringing along some papers, and they made it sort of clear their head man back to Rome has a personal interest in it. I hear tell he's some strutting banty-rooster...."

"Benito Mussolini. I met him," Horace smiled. "And you're right about that. He does remind me of a nervous rooster on a Saturday evening."

"Well, seeing as how you know him and all, and seeing as how you two are known all over the world, and since you've got your swell boat here and all, well, I was thinking that when these fellows come up from Chicago, maybe we could meet on your boat. It would be private-like and well, to tell you the truth, a lot more impressive than my office, if you get my drift."

"We can have him over for lemonade, but we're full up if you're thinking about putting him up for the night."

"Now, I didn't say anything about putting him up. Just a nice place to meet so they understand we can keep up with the big boys.

You know, class. Now look, if it turns into dinner, well, I was thinking fish might be a good idea. I don't know if they have fish over there," the chief said.

"Oh, I know for certain they're awfully fond of it in Sardinia," Horace said with a straight face. The chief missed the joke, but out of the corner of his eyes, Horace could see Theo shake his head in disgust.

Ox-Bow was practically deserted. Several of the local women were at their easels, and working with them was the young man who they assumed was Carl Hoerman. For a while Theo and Horace stood at a distance, watching them paint. "You know, I don't think there is one tree out here they haven't painted," Horace said. "Always the same – the lagoon, lower branches of the trees, and then they seem to disappear over the top of the canvas. It almost seems like everyone out here has to do it at least once."

Inside the Old Inn, Horace was surprised to see Beatrix standing in front of the painting that had kept his attention since he first saw it. She was lost in thought, and quietly noted their passing through the lounge to Harriet's office.

"Body guarding," Fred explained, as he stood up from the chair outside Harriet's office. "Since I'm supposed to be in the body-guarding business, I thought it might be a good idea to keep a look out from here. You two look okay. You can pass."

"Please tell me that it wasn't your idea to post Fred outside my door." Harriet was irritable.

"No, he must have come up with that one all on his own. He does that sort of thing once in a while. Mind you, until we know what's what, it isn't the worst of his ideas. Horace answered. "I sort of wish I'd come up with it first."

"I'm perfectly capable of looking after myself. Would you believe he wanted to stay in here with me? That's just what I don't need with all the work I've got to do," she said, looking down at a stack of papers. "Well, we managed to lose a lot of money last week, and we'll lose more this week. Six or seven students have pulled out. Cancelled completely. At this rate we can go belly up in record speed, and then I won't have to worry about resigning. There won't be anything to resign from the way this is going."

Horace ignored her and avoided the temptation of trying to make her feel better. "Has there been any more mischief-making?"

"No, thank goodness."

"Well, that's something in our favour. It might mean it was a student who's been doing it. If we're lucky, it was one of the deserters who packed it in. By the way, we just saw the chief who told us the name of the victim. He is, or rather, he was, a visiting Italian art professor from Florence named Flavio Pulchini. Does that ring a bell to you?"

Harriet looked up and said slowly, "I don't think so. Did the chief say what he was doing up here, or why he'd come up?"

"Garrison's not certain. Apparently he was in Chicago at the Art Institute, so maybe he heard about Ox-Bow and wanted to come and look around. Or, maybe he just wanted to come up here for a little jaunt and fun. No one knows yet. Maybe we'll find out more this afternoon when a man from the Italian consulate arrives."

"Must be important if they're doing that," Harriet said.

"Maybe. Or, maybe things are quiet there and they need something to do," Horace smiled.

"In the mean time, unless you object, we thought we'd look around and see if we can find something we missed," Theo added.

"No, go ahead, and do me a favour and take your watch dog with you."

When they left her office, they pulled Fred off guard duty, telling him that they needed his help outside. "Theo, I don't think I'm in Mrs. Hansen's good graces at the moment, so why don't you take the kitchen and see if you can get a handle on a serrated knife," Horace suggested.

"You're just full of them today, aren't you? That's the third one this morning," Theo fussed.

"Third what?"

"Third pun. The often-failed attempt at humour by the poorly educated."

"Highly educated," Horace corrected him. "Good luck with the old girl, and then when you finish up, we'll be down by the fire pit."

Horace and Fred were about half-way across the Meadow when Beatrix came up behind them, carrying his silver headed cane. "You must have left this in the car. Phoebe tells me you're supposed to use it until your leg gets better. Would you like to use it now?" she asked with a slight wink to remind him of their childhood game. "By the way, I'm sure you know that the head is loose. It is unique."

She joined the two men as they slowly made their way through the grass, looking down to find anything they might have missed before. When they got to the fire pit Horace said, "Now, the other night, we were all down here for the bonfire...."

"And I wandered up along the shore for a few minutes to get the smoke out of my eyes," she reminded them. The three of them followed her footprints through the sandy soil to the spot where she had been standing. Fred continued ahead of them, scouting through the tall grasses on both sides. There was nothing to indicate she had gone any farther. "Good," he said under his breath, knowing that she had been truthful.

When they made their way back to the fire pit, Horace looked towards the Old Inn. "I didn't realize it before, but it isn't possible to see the whole meadow from here. I thought it was. Thunderation! There's a blindspot." He used his walking to point to some low branches from a nearby pine tree, and the shrubs underneath it. "I thought we had a better view. But sitting here, we couldn't see the far end of the meadow. Look at how it lines up – campfire here, trees and bushes, and the building. Everything to the right is blocked. Whoever did the killing must have been up there, saw the victim pass, then circled through the blind spot."

"He must have been fairly close to you, Doctor Howell," Fred said. Her eyebrows shot up, and she shuddered at his comment. "You hear anything?" he asked. "You know, footsteps or someone pushing through the brush, something like that?" Beatrix said she had not, nor seen anything. Fred shook his head and let out a low whistle. "You could have bought the farm, you realize?"

"So, you're probably right, Beatrix, about the fellow being killed on the spot, and not dragged or carried and then dumped. You would have heard him when he dropped the body," Horace told her. "If you were to ask me, whoever did it must have worked fast to kill him, stick that palette knife in the wound, and get away without being seen. It's either an impressive piece of work or they got a very lucky break. And you're still convinced that palette knife was a calling card?"

"I think so. Yes. Yes, I am. It stands to reason. It's the only reason for it. And, it's something the Sicilian Mafia, the Black Hand and a lot of cultures do. It's a fetish, a ritual meant to send a message to the victim's family and friends," she said firmly.

"And so we circle back to the Mafia again. Fred, when we get back into town, I'd like you to keep scouting around. See if there is anything with the Chicago Mob going on. Right now, I'm going back to the boat," Horace said. He was hoping that perhaps Theo had learned something from Mrs. Hansen.

"It's like this," Theo said quietly when he sat down next to his brother. "If there's a knife missing, you'd never know it. Not the way she runs that kitchen. You know how Mrs. Garwood is as fastidious as you are when it comes to knives? Well, Mrs. Hansen is a lot more casual. She just tosses them into a drawer. If one is missing, I'm not certain even she would know it."

"Gar! Gar, where did that flag come from>" Horace shouted from the sidewalk, pointing to it as it fluttered gently over the pilot house.

The captain waited until Doctor Horace was aboard. "Well, we heard tell that the Italian ambassador is coming here for dinner, so I thought we ought to do it up proper-like to welcome him. You like it?"

"The ambassador, you say?"

"That's what I got from the shoe shine boy over to the barbershop. A man can learn a lot listening to a shoe shine boy; they get him; all sorts of news. Picked up a stock tip or two he got from a fellow who got it from his broker. Anyways, that's neither here nor there right now. The ambassador is coming all the way from Washington. He got it from Dominic who heard it from the police chief. So, I gave him a couple of bucks and his ma ran the flag up on Singer. Looks pretty good, if you don't get too close. But say, that's something, the Italian ambassador coming here! Must have heard about you meeting up Mr. Duce in Rome last year. I got to tell you, the Missus is cooking up a storm to put on a good feed for him. She's in the galley right now, so it wouldn't be wise to interrupt her."

"I see. Well, it's not an ambassador, but a man from the consulate in Chicago."

"Well, he's still pretty high up there in the ranks, isn't he? Sort of near the top man, probably."

"That's true. But Gar, that's the French flag, so take it down before anyone sees it. Thunderation!" Horace growled as he started to go to his library.

"You sure about that?"

"I'm sure. Get it down!"

"Well, I'll be. And you're out a couple of bucks, too," Gar held out his hand for the money. "Well, I'm going to hold onto it just in case some French big-wig turns up. We'll be ready for him, won't we?"

"Good thinking. And, just what is Mrs. Garwood making for dinner?"

"Good old fashioned Yankee pot roast with all the trimmings. Ought to be a real treat for everyone on account of the fact they probably can't get it over there in Italy." Gar saluted his boss. "Better get on to that flag, I guess."

Phoebe had heard her grandfather return to the boat, and quickly ran from the stern to greet him. "I heard the Italian ambassador is coming. Can I meet him, please? I've never met an ambassador before. No one in my class has ever met one, so I'll be the first! Please? I've been practicing how to courtesy, and I've got it down pat, so can I?" She carefully demonstrated her new skill.

"Well, of course you can, but he's a consulate, so he's a couple of ranks below an ambassador," he said, taking her hand as they walked into his study. "And, what you're doing is called a 'curtsy'. But now, Phoebe, just don't be surprised if he reaches out to take your hand and kisses the back of it."

"Yuck! Kiss my hand?" she crinkled up her face in disgust.

"Well, that's what happens when you're a young lady and a gentleman is introduced to you. Better get used to it if you're going to be in high society," he smiled. "Think of it as what your mother calls 'Paris Manners.'"

Phoebe frowned and thought it over. "Well, Grandfather, if Henry thinks he's going to kiss me, he's got another think coming. I'll turn his nose to twelve!"

"And who is this young man? Someone you like?"

"No! He's horrible! He's at my school and some of the other girls say he's cute, but I don't want to get kissed by him or any other boy! Not now, not ever! Yuck!" she stamped her left foot for emphasis.

"Sounds to me like you're rather sweet on him," he teased.

"I am not!" She screwed up her face as if she had just swallowed a tablespoon of castor oil. "I'm going to practice my piano!" she said as she walked off.

"Thunderation! That piano!" This time it was Doctor Horace who screwed up his face. "Yuck, is right!" He closed the study door behind her.

When Mrs. Hansen came to give Phoebe her lesson, Fred knocked on the door. "Thought this might be a good time to do a little more scouting around, maybe for the next hour, if you get my drift," he said solemnly, nodding in the general direction of the music.

"I can't blame you, Fred. Wait a minute. I want you to smell this," Horace said, handing him the hip flask Pauline had given him the night of the murder. "You don't have to taste it. Smell it and tell me what you think."

Fred's nose wrinkled. "Smells like fuel oil laced with honey. That some new medicine or something? Anything that stinks like that must cure something."

"More like something. Now Fred, as long as Mrs. Hansen's here for the next hour, I'd like you to drive to her place and have a look-see. She keeps bees, so watch yourself. But see if there is anything strange going on out there."

"Bees? I'd sooner face Hindenburg's whole army than a flock of bees. That important, is it?"

"That important. Just go out there and see if there's something unusual. You don't have to get up close, and get out of there within the hour. And then get back here and cleaned up for dinner. We got guests coming."

"Yeah, I heard. Il Duce himself is coming. Got that from a fellow at the filling station."

"Il Duce, you say?"

"Yup. Bet he'll be real happy to see you again, Doc. Say, Doc, you keep that old battleaxe busy for an hour. I don't want to get caught between her and the bees."

Horace promised he would.

Late in the afternoon the police chief brought the consul, Nino Giori, to the *Aurora*, along with Doctor Landis. After the introductions and formal greetings, all of them went over the autopsy report. Giori slowly read through it, periodically asking Doctor Landis to explain a medical term. "And this scar on his left hip? How might you account for that?" he asked the physician.

"I don't. It's a number of years old, well healed, but the scar is still visible. Perhaps an accident. Perhaps, if he was in the war....? Maybe something else. It might even be from childhood. I noticed it so I put it on the report. The only thing I can say for certain is that it had no bearing on the cause of the death. You see, at the time of the autopsy we didn't know the man's identity, and sometimes old scars can help identify the deceased."

"Yes, yes, of course," the consul said quietly. "You must be thorough, of course, as are our great physicians in Rome." He quietly closed the folder and thanked all of them. "Now, captain, I will ask for your assistance in making arrangements for the body to be sent by rail to await the instructions of the family. And, I will then leave you to get on with your investigation and find the murderer of one of Italy's most notable professors of art. We will, of course, be closely following your progress, and I assure you, we put ourselves and our resources at your disposal should you need our assistance in bringing this sad affair to a most successful conclusion."

"Thank you," the chief said quietly, relieved that all had gone well. Almost, as if on cue, Mrs. Garwood came out from the galley to suggest to Doctor Horace that they move into the dining room for dinner.

Giori stood up and walked to Mrs. Garwood, clicked his heals, bowed, and kissed her hand. "Thank you, my most gracious lady, but I have already accepted an invitation by your Captain of Police to dine with him. I had mentioned my desire to taste the whitefish of this most enchanting region and he has honoured me by making it so." He moved around the room, saying his farewells to each person. Phoebe curtsied and swallowed hard as she felt him take her hand to kiss it.

"You know, I would be honoured if you would include me. I'd like to learn more about the state of affairs in Italy. I met Il Duce in Rome last year," Horace said suddenly. Captain Garrison looked surprised, and realized he was obligated to extend the invitation.

Doctor Horace didn't see the scowl that swept across Mrs. Garwood's face.

Theo was still waiting up for him in the library when Horace returned a few hours later. "Well, that was quite the show you put on. You beat all, you know that? I've known you to be arrogant, demanding, insulting and just plain rude to people, but never to your staff. This was sure a new one, even for you. You really hurt Mrs. Garwood walking out on a meal like that. I trust your precious whitefish was worth it!" he snapped.

"Thunderation!" Horace smiled. "I didn't give two raps about the fish. I wanted to listen to those two and find out what they're up to. That's the reason I took a powder and ducked out like that. I smell a rat in this whole thing, and the best way to get a man to drop his guard is over food. And, here's the real kicker. We got to the restaurant and our chief gives a wink-wink nod-nod to the waiter and orders their special Italian coffee. That's what he called it – Italian Coffee. Well, let me tell you, I've had a lot of coffee in my day, and I've never seen red coffee. And, you know why? It was wine, and that means our chief knows all about what's going on around here. Sit down, there's more to tell you."

"What?"

"For starters, the chief is playing this whole thing out as nothing more than a robbery gone wrong. That's been his story from the start and he wants to stick to it. He wants us and everyone else to believe this Professor Pulchini must have gone out to Ox-Bow to look around, and someone must have figured he was carrying a lot of money on him. Well, maybe he was and maybe he wasn't. Garrison's convinced someone must have seen him flashing it around town and followed him out there. Either he wants a quick and easy answer, no matter what the truth is, or he's covering something up."

"Well, a robbery makes sense to me," Theo said slowly. "Face it, it is a possibility."

"I was open to that idea, but I'm not now. Not at all, and here's why. I was sitting where I could see Giori reading the autopsy papers, and it wasn't the same report we signed. The papers we signed included mention of the palette knife, remember? Well, this one didn't mention the palette knife. It was left out!"

Theo blew the air out of his cheeks. "You sure about that?"

"Positive. And remember how we initialled each page. Well, on that page it wasn't your handwriting. You always have a little flip at the start of the "T". That page didn't have it. The others did, but not that page. It was forged! And, there's got to be a reason for it!" Horace slammed his fist down on his desk.

"You're sure about that?" his brother asked.

"Absolutely!"

"So, what's their game? And why?"

Horace smiled. "Now, that's the question. We don't know who did it, the forgery, although it has to be either Landis or Garrison. The chief took the papers with him, so maybe he did it. Or, maybe he made Landis do it, willingly or under duress."

"Maybe a pay-off, you think?" Theo asked.

The two men sat in silence, long enough for Horace to fill his pipe. "Two possibilities. The first is that Landis bent the evidence to make it look like it was just a robbery gone wrong. There wasn't a watch or a wallet on him, so it stands to reason. Maybe Garrison will catch the person who did it, maybe not. Maybe that's all there is to it, but I don't think so."

Theo interrupted: "Why?"

"Simple. It's a small town. People in small towns, especially tourist towns, don't want it to get around that people get murdered there. It's bad for business. They can't keep it out of the newspaper, but they can keep it off the front page above the fold. That's why these papers put all the society news on the front page: Mrs. GotRocks hosted Miss Prunella Jones who just returned home from visiting her sixth cousin twice removed. Things like that. A real news article gets buried inside one week, and that's it, and everyone gets on with life. After the holiday-makers go home at the end of summer, then perhaps a bit more of the story."

Theo considered that for a while. "And what's your other theory?"

"Well, remember Beatrix saying it was a calling card from a paid killer? Garrison and Landis both heard her say it. If Giori thought a hit man had assassinated Pulchini, then it might have gotten kicked upstairs to the State Department and they'd be sticking their noses in it. Or, the Italians might kick up a stink and cause more problems. And maybe, just maybe, this Pulchini was on the outs with old Musso, and that's why he was killed, and maybe Giori told the chief he didn't want it to look like anything other than a robbery and murder. If that's what happened, I hope the chief at least did get a pay-off. And a big one!

"Whatever it is, something stinks. Just plain stinks!" Horace said.

Theo got up and stared silently out the library window, looking at the river. "I don't like this," Theo said. "You might be letting your imagination run away with you. You know that, don't you? Maybe we should just stay out of this and let Garrison handle it. We're surgeons, not detectives, and we don't want to get into some dicey international affairs. I just don't like this. Any of it. Not at all." After a while he turned around. "Well, I'm going to bed, not that I'm likely to get much sleep. Between what you found out and Mrs. Garwood's dinner...."

Horace winced. "I'll have to patch that up, won't I?"

"Yup. Well, if it's any comfort, you didn't miss much of a meal. You remember Mother's pot roast? Well, Mrs. G used her old recipe."

"I am sorry to hear that. Left-overs, I presume?"

"Yeah."

Theo walked slowly back to his cabin, thinking over what his brother had told him. It didn't bother him that Garrison was well aware of the booze flowing in town. After all, he and Horace were just barely skirting the law by writing prescriptions for themselves. But it was the change in the autopsy report that was troubling. Why would Garrison or Landis change it and forge their initials?

Half an hour later, he was wide awake, still turning it over in his mind, when he realized there was a third possibility: Beatrix. She could have had a hand in it, just as easily as the others. And maybe she was the killer and somehow finagled the forgery.

CHAPTER NINE

Fred knocked on the library door a little after nine the next morning. Horace called for him to come in, then added, "and close the door, for heaven's sake. Phoebe's practicing her clinkers again."

"I'll say one thing, she's sure consistent about hitting the sour notes."

Horace beckoned him to sit down. "Did you find out anything?"

"Plenty. That's why I didn't get back here for dinner. I guess you took a powder and missed it too, which from what I heard isn't going over any too well with Mrs. G. Anyways, I got it on good authority over to the Green Parrot that there was an Italian fellow who came in on the North America the other day. He was dressed up like a real swell, and stuck out like that sore thumb of mine you dressed a few years back. Brown leather suitcase and wearing a suit and tie. Up here in a resort town, if you can believe it. Now, if you were to ask me, someone fancied up like that must have given someone the idea he was going to be easy pickings, being a foreigner and all. He came into the Green Parrot and asked the girl behind the counter where he could find a room, and she told him of a place over on Park Street. From what I can figure, he got in a taxi and rented a place up near the water works for a couple of nights."

"Good work, Fred. That confirms what we know. Good."

"Yeah, well there's plenty more. I done did what you said about wandering around and came across this fellow down to the park with a cribbage board, and we played a couple of games. Turns out, he's the landlord at the place where this fellow who got himself killed stayed, and he told me that the dead man pulled out his wallet, and it was loaded with cash. So, there you got it. Robbery and murder, easy as pie. And say, this fellow might be all right as a landlord, but I double-skunked him both games and took a buck a game off him. Now, I know the Good Book doesn't approve of gambling, but since I made two bucks off of him, I figure if I was to put one in the collection plate come Sunday, everything would more or less be jake."

"Interesting. Now, tell me, did you get out to Mrs. Hansen's place?" Horace asked.

"Sure did," Fred reported. "There's plenty fishy going on out there. She's got these three beehives out back of her place, sort of in a big triangle. You could see bees going in and out all the time. And, it weren't just bees coming and going. Right in the middle of where she got those hives, there was a hole in the ground with a ladder sticking out. Some fellow named 'Red' – that's what they were calling him, Red, was carrying boxes of jars to hand down to a fellow in the hole. And then they hauled up some other boxes of jars and put them on the back of a truck. When they were done, they pulled out the ladder, put down some boards and covered them up with dirt, and then they put a big work table over all of that. Not a fancy one; more like a workbench a gardener uses.

"There's some funny doings over to her place, and that's for sure. I didn't stick around too long to see where the truck got to, and figured it was best to hightail it out of there before Old Iron Pants came home.. I can go back out there, if you want me to."

"I do! And I also want you to see if you can find out something about this fellow Red, you mentioned. And, see if he's got some friends."

Fred smiled. "Only thing I like better than winning at cribbage is poking into places my nose doesn't belong. He got up, stepping past Theo as he came into the study.

"I take it you still think we ought to be involved in this?" Theo asked.

"Yes," Horace said firmly. "There is something very strange about this business, and we both know it. For whatever reason, Garrison or Landis is whitewashing this. I think they hope in a few days it will all be conveniently forgotten. Or, they're getting pressure from the Italians. The other possibility is that the mayor wants this played low key. Two murders in two years isn't good for business in a little burgh like this."

"I've sort of been thinking the same thing. And, maybe there's another reason, too. Whatever it might be, you realize if we keep stirring the pot like this, we're not going to make ourselves very popular around here," Theo reminded him.

"I'm not trying to win a popularity contest!" Horace shot back at him.

"Good, because you'd come in dead last place every time. Speaking of popularity, you haven't gotten around to fix things up with Mrs. G yet."

"The next thing on my list," Horace smiled, opening the container and taking out two pills.

"And what are those for?" Theo asked.

"Something Beatrix gave me. Helps me focus."

"Something Beatrix gave you? You think that's wise? She's still a suspect in my book."

"It's a formula she worked on in her lab, and thinks it might work."

"Right. Something she says she makes in her lab. Well, that makes it perfectly alright then, doesn't it?" Theo's voice was sarcastic. "You might as well know, I don't trust that woman. She could be the murderer, and I think she is dangerous. There. You heard it, and I don't care if you like it or not. "Don't forget Mrs. G. I mean it," Theo said as he made his way out of the library.

He went over to the rail to look out, horrified at what he had just seen. Beatrix had found Horace's weak spot. If a bathing beauty from Atlantic City or a Hollywood actress knocked on his door he wouldn't notice. Clara Bow could pout her lips, Annette Henning could sing, Gloria Swanson could flash her smile at him, and he'd be clueless. He wouldn't know if a woman was flirting with him or not. But let some woman with brains walk through the door…. Theo knew he had to do something before Horace was the next man with a palette knife stuck through his chest. He slammed his right fist on the railing. The woman was dangerous. He smiled and chuckled, "And when she smiles, she could be rather fetching," he told himself, then looked around to be sure no one overheard him.

"And just how was your whitefish last evening, Doctor Balfour? Perfectly satisfying and more enjoyable than your sainted mother's recipe for pot roast?" Mrs. Garwood asked icily as he stood in the doorway of the galley.

"Well, let's just say that the fish tasted better last night than the crow I'm eating right now. I am truly sorry for being so rude and thoughtless by walking out on your dinner like that, Mrs. G. What I did was wrong and insulting to you. I hope you'll accept my apology," he said quietly.

"And since you had your fish last night, I'm quite certain you wouldn't want it two days running, now will you?" she asked.

"No, and it was very kind of you to ask. I assure you I shall enjoy whatever you put in front of me," he smiled. He thought of his mother's cooking and added, "and eat it with relish."

"Then you'll be happy to know that we're having left-overs to-night. I had plenty of it left from last night, and waste not want not. Mrs. Hansen gave me a new recipe for making it into hash which we will be having tomorrow night as well.

"Harriet, I apologize for interrupting you," Beatrix said as she stood in the doorway of the office, "but can you tell me something about the painting, the Italian one in the lounge? It has been on my mind for several days. I've been meaning to ask, but you seem a bit preoccupied. Do you know anything about it, or even where it came from?"

"I really can't tell you very much. And, as you just said, I haven't had time to look into it more closely. It's been a very busy time around here," Harriet answered as she picked up some papers on her desk, holding them in hopes that her friend would take the hint and understand she was still busy, and didn't want to spend time chatting. "There are some art history books in the library. You might try them; they might help. And let me know if you find out something important."

"Yes, yes, of course I will. It's such an interesting painting. I was just hoping to learn a bit more, that is all. Mr. Reynolds told me how it came here. Do paintings often appear out of the thin air like that?"

"Well, it may surprise you, but yes, it does happen. Sometimes, someone loans us a painting from their collection, or they'll donate one. Or, Mr. Fursman or one of the Chicago teachers will borrow one from the archives. Meanwhile.... Whatever you can find out...." Harriet waved the papers to signal the conversation was over.

"Thank you. I'll see if I can find anything more. Then we can properly curate it."

Her final comment did not endear her to Harriet, but she said nothing. Curate it properly. Sure. Of course, right away. And I'll do that right after we find the murderer, figure out who did the vandalism, find some way to pay the bills, get more students and do something about that crazy lady teaching my daughter piano lessons.

Beatrix returned to the lounge for the third time that morning, once again standing in front of the painting, studying it. She heard a car door slam and wheeled around. Fred was sitting on a chair near the car.

"I need your help," she said firmly after she went outside.

"What's wrong, Doctor Howell?"

"I need you to drive me into town right away. And, can you open the trunk for me? It is important."

He smiled. "Just about to go back into town, anyway. Doctor Theo and his missus will be back in a few minutes. I was about to drive them in. The boss is waiting on the boat, probably reading or something." He nodded toward the general direction of the fire pit near the lagoon. "They're down there, still looking around for something, I'd guess."

"Good. Open the trunk for me, please. And, you must not say a word to anyone! Not a word!"

Beatrix dashed back into the inn, looked around the lounge to make sure no one was nearby, and took the painting off the wall and hurried out of the building. To her relief, no one had seen or heard her. When she got to the car and saw an old horse blanket in the trunk, she quickly wrapped it around the frame. "Not a word!" she repeated as Fred closed the trunk. Theo and Clarice had started back up across the meadow.

"We were feeding the carp," Clarice said. "Some of them are quite large."

"They've got some big snapping turtles there. Your mother ever make turtle soup, Fred? Now, you two, don't you dare say anything about this to anyone, but seeing those fish made me realize that Horace isn't the only one who has a taste for whitefish. Fred, when we get into town, drop us off somewhere so we can have lunch," Theo said smugly.

"And then, would you drop me off at the boat, please?" Beatrix added as she slipped into the passenger's seat, her face set firmly ahead. Fred took them down the rough gravel and dirt road from Ox-Bow back into town. Just as they passed the brick waterworks building an old pickup truck came up fast behind them, almost riding on the car's bumper. Beatrix gasped in fear, certain that someone knew she had taken the painting and was following them. "Must be some fool in a rush to get himself killed," Fred muttered as the truck went around them, spraying exhaust and gravel. By the time they got to Douglas, they saw the driver parked at the pumps of the filling station, waiting for the attendant. Beatrix breathed in relief. It wasn't anyone she had seen at Ox-Bow.

Clarice and Theo got out in front of the Post Office, saying that they would find a place to eat. "And remember, we're keeping this a secret between the four of us, right?" Theo reminded them. "Especially from Mrs. G."

A few minutes later Beatrix practically ran up the gangplank to find Horace. Less than a minute later the two of them hurried back down and got into the backseat of the car. "Fred, you know where I parked my plane? Good. Let's go!"

"Beatrix, I thought you said we are going to the hospital," Horace asked in surprise.

"We are. The one in Grand Rapids."

"Well, we can drive there. We don't need to...."he started to object.

"No, we can't. The plane will be faster, and this way Fred can buy us some time." She leaned forward to tell Fred, "And this way, Fred, you will not have to tell any lies. Just do not give any answers. At least not for as long as possible. Stall. We need a couple of hours. After that, it will no longer matter. No! That is not right. Fred, do not say anything to anyone!"

Fred looked into the rear view mirror for some indication from his employer. Doctor Horace grimly nodded in agreement. Neither man dared ask what Beatrix was planning.

"Have you ever flown before, Horace?" Beatrix asked as she and Fred pulled the canvas off the cockpit.

"No, and I'm too old to start now and too young to get killed in one of these contraptions!"

"Never mind that. You will not get killed in an aeroplane when I am flying. Good. This will be a new experience for you. Now, just get in. Pull yourself up and step in." She turned toward Fred. "I saw some baling twine in the trunk. Please tie that around the blanket and picture. Nice and tight."

She turned to watch Horace start to get into the rear seat of the Stearman, and laughed. "If you have never been in an aeroplane before, then you have never flown one have you?. You are not taking your first lesson from me. That is my seat. You fly up in front."

"How can you see from back there?" he protested.

"Trust me. I can. Now, front seat, and there is a leather helmet on the seat. Put it on, and pull the straps tight. I will strap you in after I check the plane."

Fred finished tying the painting and handed it up to Horace. "Boss, sure looks like you're ready to take on the Red Baron and the rest of the flying Huns," he teased.

"Very funny," Horace snarled. "Since this thing isn't equipped with a machine gun, go find some rocks so I can throw at them."

He remained in a foul mood as Beatrix tightened the straps of his harness. "Quit fussing unless you want to fall out! Sit still and quit fidgeting," she said firmly. His foul mood slipped into sheer fear.

"You got a map or something to get you there?" Fred called up from the ground.

"We will not need one. We will follow the road up to the train tracks, then follow the tracks north and east. At our altitude we will see where we need to go. Now, Horace, signal with your hands. Left or right. Hand out, point down if you see something down there is something I should see. Understand?"

"Understood," Horace croaked out.

"Oh, one more thing. If you see another aeroplane coming straight at us, wave both hands over your head so I can get out of the way before we crash." Beatrix tightened her lips to hide a smile. "You had better duck, too, so I can see over your head."

"Fred, once we are in the air, I want you to go for a drive. Get on the road and go as far south as Pier Cove. Keep your eyes open for someone following you. If you think someone is behind you, drive on down to South Haven. Nice and steady, like a Sunday drive. If there is still someone behind you when you get to South Haven, shake them off your tail and come back to Saugatuck as fast as you can and pull up in front of the police department. That should be your safest bet. Is that clear?"

He snapped to attention and saluted. "Yes, Ma'am. A diversionary tactic to draw the enemy off our front!"

Beatrix set the fuel mixture and spark, instructing Fred to stand behind the propeller to turn over the engine. "Again!" she shouted for the fourth time, fearing that the plane wouldn't start. It would dash her plans before they even got started. Finally the engine coughed and sputtered to life. She let it warm up, adjusting the fuel, feathering the throttle as the engine revved up to full power, and signalled Fred to pull out the chocks. With a wave and a point to his car and another wave to tell him to get it off the field, she taxied to the far end, turned, and waited. A final look at the gauges, the engine at full power, and she raced down the field and took to the air.

From five hundred feet, Horace could easily see everything on the ground, including people who were shading their eyes as they looked up to see them. A few waved. Horace didn't wave back. He was holding on to the plane for dear life.

Beatrix circled over Saugatuck and Douglas, then flew over the *Aurora* to follow the Kalamazoo River out to the lake. Below them were fishing boats, a few runabouts, and sailboats. All of it was lost on Horace who was desperately trying not to get sick. He jumped and strained against the harness every time the plane made so much as a twitch, gasping in terror the two times the engine coughed. He wasn't able to see Beatrix behind him – smiling and laughing as she enjoyed the freedom of being in the air. "Thank you One-Eyed Wiley!" she shouted in pure joy.

She took them north along the coast, then dipped the right wings as she banked sharply to the right when they passed over the lighthouse at the entrance to the harbour. Horace tried shouting and waving to get her attention, to let her know it wasn't Grand Rapids. She ignored him, looking for the landing field north of the city. It wasn't until she landed and turned off the engine that Horace twisted around to shout, "We're in Holland, not Grand Rapids! Wrong place!"

She had taxied up to a small shack where two young men came jogging toward her plane waiting for the propeller to stop spinning. Beatrix intentionally waited for the right moment so she could see the look of surprise that always came when she pulled off her helmet and shook out her grey hair. Like all of the others, these two men were not expecting a woman. "Afternoon gentlemen," she said. "Do me a favor please. Put some fuel in the tank, please. And, help my friend down. He may be a bit shaky. It is his first flight. Now, do you have a telephone. I need to call for a taxi."

"I can run you into town," one of the men said.

"Then to the hospital, please," Beatrix said as they got into a Ford pickup. "We'll be there about an hour. I'd like you to wait for us. Will five dollars now and five more when we get back here be acceptable?

"Lady," the young man grinned. "For ten bucks, take two hours. Take all afternoon. You're the first girl flier I've ever seen."

She thanked him for the compliment, knowing she was old enough to be his grandmother.

Theo and Clarice walked slowly back to the boat, both of them yawning after a substantial lunch. "I think I'm going to take a beauty nap, even if you do say I'm already quite beautiful," she giggled, squeezing his hand.

"You do that. I'm going to go over to the Maplewood Hotel to make a telephone call. Just to check on how things are back home."

When Theo came out of the hotel he staggered to a bench, his mind reeling.

CHAPTER TEN

"I would like to borrow your lab and assistant for a few minutes, perhaps a bit longer, but that remains to be seen. I will also need a high powered microscope and some slides, and do tell me you have a modern x-ray machine," Beatrix said after Horace had made their introductions to a receptionist who had called the hospital administrator. The man smiled and said they had carte blanche for whatever they needed. "It's quite the honour for us to have the Doctors Balfour in our hospital," he smiled. "Yes, quite the little coup for our hospital!" He turned to the receptionist and added, "Do let the Sentinel know about these two world famous doctors visiting here."

"Doctors Balfour and Howell," Horace corrected him.

"I do not think this will take us very long," Beatrix said flatly as they walked behind him through the corridors to the laboratory.

Beatrix put the painting face down on a lab table. "First, a little surgery. You will assist, Doctor Balfour. We begin by removing the painting from the frame. I know this is a hospital, but we will need a screw driver, pliers, and a small hammer." The lab assistant went to the janitor's closet to get the tools.

"First assistant? Haven't done that for a few years. Well, unless I am assisting Theo," Horace smiled. Beatrix ignored him, her eyes focused on her work.

"Whoever did this knew what they were doing, using wedges rather than nails or brads to hold the painting in the frame. Well done, but a bit too tight to be old. The wood should have dried out by now and loose. There is our first clue, Doctor," she said.

"Unless it was recently reframed," Horace suggested. She ignored him.

She worked silently, expertly prying the edges out from two adjacent sides with some effort, then carefully lifted out the painting. Beatrix held it up, inspecting the front, then turning it to look at the edges. She said nothing, and Horace had no idea what she was hoping to find. "Scalpel, then hold the Petri dish directly under where I am working. Time to do a small biopsy. No, two biopsies, perhaps more."

Horace was horrified as she scraped a few flakes of red paint off the edge of the canvas. "Another dish," she said, this time scraping off some brown paint.

"You're ruining a precious painting!" he protested.

Beatrix looked up and tightened her lips. "Perhaps, but I doubt it. In fact, I am quite sure I am not. When we put it back into the frame no one will notice the scraping. Even if they do, no one will know when the damage was done. They will assume it was scraped by the framer. Considering the age someone hopes we will assign to the painting, it would have been in and out of frames many times, each of them a possible opportunity to do slight damage. It will not matter. Good, we have enough samples. And now we prepare the slides. First lesson in forensic art pathology."

She turned to the lab assistant. "Will you take the painting down to the x-ray department and have several exposures done. I need images from various parts of the painting, but especially near the centre." She pointed to several areas of importance to her. "A good clear resolution at maximum magnitude. Thank you. And, please stay with the painting and do not let it out of your sight. Once the plates are dry, bring them back with the painting, please."

She said nothing more as she mounted the two slides, one for each color, carefully using the scalpel to separate the flakes of paint. "And now, we get to see what's here." She pushed the first slide onto the microscope plate, turned the mirror beneath it to better reflect the light, and adjusted the lenses to set the focus. She bent over it, studying it for well over a minute before she looked up. "And, it is just as I expected. Look at this, Doctor Balfour." Beatrix stepped aside to make room for Horace.

"What am I looking for?" he asked.

"Minute pieces of iron or hematite crystals. You should have no difficulty recognizing them by their uniformity."

He adjusted the focus, studying the slide far longer than had Beatrix, before standing up. "Either I don't know what I'm looking for, or I'm not seeing anything."

"Fortunately, you're not seeing anything I just described. I will explain later. And now the brown." She repeated the process, saying nothing as she examined the sample, then turned the microscope over to Horace. She smiled. "On this slide do you see any small irregular pieces of brown?"

"No, should I?" he asked.

"Yes, but like the red paint on slide one, they aren't there. In the Renaissance, when this picture was supposedly painted, painters, or more likely their assistances or apprentices, made their own pigment. Red was invariably made from hematite – iron in layman's terms. They pulverized it for hours, ground it, and made it into a fine dust. The powder would be carefully mixed with linseed oil to make the pigment. Brown came from crushed beetles. Again, the same method. In both cases, no matter how hard they crushed them, there should still be microscopic fragments. They are not present here on either slide."

"Which means?" he asked.

"Which means this is a modern painting done with commercially manufactured paint, using pigment and turpentine or one of its derivatives. It is fairly safe to propose that this painting is no more than a century ago, and perhaps less. We could be far more certain if we could do a chemical analysis."

"But the paint is dried out and cracked," he objected.

"Ah, the marvels of the modern kitchen stove. Turn the temperature down as low as it will go, watch it carefully, and bake until done. I suspect it was an electric stove."

Horace couldn't resist asking, "Why?"

"I'll show you later."

"So, is it a forgery?" he asked.

"That's a legal question, and I am not saying that. I am saying it is modern. It would be forgery if someone tried passing it off as an old painting. Students copy old paintings all the time to learn their style and technique. It depends on the intent of the artist. Meanwhile, we will preserve these slides. If there was criminal intent, our slides will serve as evidence. I take it you remember how to preserve a dry slide," she teased.

They finished their work with fifteen minutes to spare before the lab assistant and an x-ray technician came in the door. "Never did an x-ray on a painting before. I don't know, but I think I might have done it wrong," the woman said. "I hope not," she apologized.

"Let's see," Beatrix answered.

She held the first plate to the window for better light, then looked at four more. She turned to the woman from the x-ray department. "No, you did it quite perfectly. Nice clear images. Well done. Thank you."

"Well?" Horace asked.

"Exactly as I suspected once you pointed the picture out to me. It is a modern painting. And, I believe it was done within the last fifty years. Whoever did this painted over another painting. Look, you can see the original. It is a waterfalls."

"What are those specks? Horace asked, using a pen to point at them.

"They are the key, Doctor Balfour, to setting the age of this painting. The key to an interesting little puzzle. Those are bits of mica. I am quite sure of it. I know of only one painter who used mica to interpret water coming off the rocks. He was a Hungarian immigrant named Henrich Schmedilak who lived near Rhinelander, Wisconsin, and died before the turn of the century. So, the painting is less than fifty years old, perhaps forty. Mica is the fingerprint!" she clapped her hands in delight. She was smiling broadly. "If this is an attempt at forgery, whoever did this was very careless or exceedingly arrogant. Then again, if the intent was not forgery, the painter simply painted over an old painting. Such things happen all the time."

Horace knew Beatrix would have continued her explanations, but she was interrupted.

"There is something else we saw on the bottom inside of the wooden frame," the woman from the x-ray department said. "Let me show you." She stood the canvas up, the painting facing away from them, and pointed to some very small letters. "You almost need a magnifying glass to see it, and it's obscured by the grain." She read the letters, "D, U, X. Dux. Any ideas."

"Probably the man who built the frame," Horace said.

"It is immaterial to your discovery of the letters, but properly, these are stretcher bars. That is not important. The letters....." Beatrix froze over, not finishing her sentence, and suddenly looking very pale. "Perhaps.... No! We must be going. Ready, Doctor Balfour?" She was out the door, leaving him to thank the staff for their help.

"So, what does all that mean?" he asked Beatrix when he caught up with her in the hall.

"As Sherlock Homes would, say, 'that's a three pipe question.'"

"What is it dear? Are you feeling alight? You look like you've seen a ghost." Clarice said after Theo came into their cabin and sat down hard on the edge of their bed. "The children! Don't tell me something has happened!"

"No, not at all," he said firmly.

"Well? What? Tell me!"

"To start off with, I didn't call home. I've been turning some things over in my mind, so I called the laboratory where Beatrix said she worked, and talked to the director, Doctor Sackett. You met Lester a few years back at a convention in Chicago."

"And?"

"And, he told me she did work there. Past tense. Used to work there. She retired about five years ago, but stayed on for another year or so to finish up some projects. She hasn't worked there since."

"Theo, that's not surprising. She and Horace are the same age, so she would have retired. Not everyone hangs on like you two, you know."

"I know. So, I asked him what he knew about her."

"And?"

"Nothing. Absolutely nothing unless it had to do with her work. She'd been there when he came. Never once did she mention a family, friends, never socialized with anyone in the lab. No pictures on her desk. Never talked about hobbies or interests or friends outside of work. If she had a life outside of her work, she never told anyone about it. Not a thing. He said she would come in every morning, work, go home, and no one saw her until the next day."

"That is strange. No department parties or dances, where she went to church, if she had a man in her life?" Clarice asked, her voice rising in fear of something wrong.

"Absolutely nothing."

"That is strange," she repeated.

"That's what Sackett said, too. People gave her a wide berth because of it. He said she wasn't rude or arrogant, just that she didn't connect with people. Some of them tried, but after a while they gave up. Well, you've seen what she is like the last few days."

"Did he tell you what she's done since she retired?"

Theo gave his wife a withering look. "No. No one knows. She's a completely closed book. You've seen the way she is. She'll talk for a few minutes if it's something that interests her, then she switches off her personality and, well, retreats into her own world. And you might as well know, she's somehow talked Horace into taking some sort of nostrum she cooked up."

"What do you mean?"

"I'm not certain. But you know how he constantly reads and re-reads those Sherlock Holmes stories. Well, he's got some new hobby horse about something called Royal Jelly. It pops up in the books, and I guess he and Conan Doyle talked about it. He's obsessed with it. Yesterday, he sent Fred out to look at Mrs. Hansen's beehives. He's up to something, and she's leading him on."

"You're not comfortable about it," she said.

"No! I am not! Ever since he came out of the hospital a few weeks ago he's been obsessed about becoming forgetful, and you know, going into a second childhood like your aunt. It's had him worried, so...... Where is my brother, by the way? I want to talk to him."

"I don't know. He wasn't here when I came back. Mrs. Garwood said that Beatrix came running up to the boat and practically dragged him away with her, and that Fred drove them off somewhere. I don't think they're back yet."

Theo pulled himself to his feet and went out on the deck, just as Fred was pulling up. "Fred, where did you take Horace and Beatrix? And more importantly, where are they now?"

"Well, I'm not supposed to say nothing to nobody about it," Fred said.

"No. I need to know. It's important. VERY important!"

"You mind if I sit down, on account of the fact that it might be a bit of a long story?"

Theo pointed to a deck chair.

CHAPTER ELEVEN

"Well, it's like this," Fred said, "and I shouldn't be saying nothing on account of the fact that I'm sworn to top secrecy. I dropped you and your missus off downtown like you said you wanted me to do, and I brought Doctor Howell back here like she said she wanted me to do. Now, she jumps out of the car and runs up to get Doctor Horace. Oh, let me back up, she had this painting with her that she got out to Ox-Bow, and then she told me to take them to the airfield because they were going up to the hospital in Grand Rapids with no map nor nothing. Just following the road, sort of like the way Rickenbacker and his boys done when they were chasing the Red Baron.

"The queer thing is, she told me to drive down to Pier Cove to make sure nobody was following me, which they weren't, and then to drive around a bit, which I done. Right after that they took off, and that's the last I saw of them. So, I did what they said and now I'm back here. Don't worry, nobody's tailing me.

"And don't you worry, Doctor Horace is strapped in good and tight so he wouldn't fall out of the plane."

Theo held up his hand to stop Fred. "Did you strap Horace in? Or, did Beatrix? Did you see him strapped in?"

"She did it. Said she wanted to see to it herself, and I figured she knew more about it than me. But he was trussed in good and tight when they took off. Why?"

"Because something isn't right. A lot of things aren't right and to begin with Horace is a blasted fool going up in an aeroplane with that crazy woman!"

"What are you talking about dear?" Clarice asked as she joined them.

"I think Horace is up flying around with our killer. Well, least who I think is the killer. It won't surprise me if Beatrix is the one who killed that fellow at Ox-Bow. Remember how she slipped away the night it happened? Then she knew all about the palette knife thing when we found the body. And when Doctor Landis brought the papers over, Horace said the autopsy report was changed and our initials forged. Then, I found out she's giving Horace some sort of medicine, and now she's got him up in her plane. I won't be surprised to find out that she flipped the plane over somewhere out over the lake and drowned him. She could be anywhere by now!"

The color drained from Clarice's face. "Now what?" she barely whispered.

Theo looked at her with anger and frustration. "I have no idea. None. What? Call the police? Call the Coast Guard? And then tell them what? That my brother and a crazy lady went for a joy ride in her plane and I'm the only one who thinks she's a murder suspect? Fat lot of good that will do us!" He threw up his hands in frustration.

The three adults had not seen Phoebe slip up quietly on the deck. Suddenly she burst into tears, wailing loudly in fear and despair. Clarice hurried to comfort her. "I'm sure it is nothing. Nothing at all. Just some confusion. Sometimes adults get confused, so there is nothing for you to worry about. I promise. Everything will be all right, and we'll laugh about this tonight. You'll see."

"I want my mother!" the girl cried all the louder, shaking and sobbing.

Clarice took charge. "Fred, you will drive us out to Ox-Bow. And not one word out of you. Not a single word to anyone! Is that clear?" she demanded.

He nodded his head, and pulled the car keys out of his pocket. Fred tried to make sense of it, but it was beyond him. Everyone seemed to be blaming him for doing what he'd been told to do. All he did was drive them out to the airfield.

From far in the distance, somewhere to the north, just as Fred was holding open the car door for her, Phoebe thought she heard the sound of an engine. Clarice thought it was nothing more than wishful thinking on the girl's part. Then she could hear something. It didn't sound like any of the boats that went up and down the river, and it was too loud to be coming from the lake. Desperate and silently praying, Phoebe scanned the sky, looking for it. Fred and Clarice joined her, all three of them holding a hand to shield their eyes as they tried to find the source of the sound.

"There!" Phoebe pointed. "Let it be Grandfather! Please, let it be grandfather!" she pleaded out loud. The wait for the plane to come into sight was agony.

"Look! There it is! It's yellow. It's Beatrix's yellow plane!" the girl shrieked in joy.

They watched from the sidewalk, Theo from above them up on the deck. "It's them! It's them! Everything is going to be okay!" Phoebe shouted, cheering and crying for joy, and hugging Fred and her aunt. "Let's go meet them!"

The plane came up the river, levelling off as it neared Saugatuck, and just before they flew over the *Aurora*, Beatrix wiggle-wagged the wings, waved, and flew on to the landing field. They could see Horace sitting stiffly upright, his face straight ahead.

"Yes, Sir!" Fred shouted. "They had good hunting! Sure looks that way."

"Grandfather's back safe and sound!" Phoebe cheered.

"I can't really see what all the fussing is about," Horace said, smiling as he went into the library, the rest of his family and Fred and Beatrix trailing behind him. "I'm certainly of an age to do what I want to do. And, I guess if I want to spend an afternoon with an old friend, there shouldn't be a problem with that, now should there?. Theo, I would have told you, but there wasn't time. Besides, you weren't even here!" He sat down in his desk chair and sighed. "Much better than that hard seat in the plane."

"And lower to the ground, too," Phoebe said, coming over to give him a hug.

"Horace, spending the afternoon with an old friend is one thing. If you even had any friends, that is. Spending it with her up in the sky in that flying machine is quite another. And, not telling us, or anyone else for that matter, anything about it, well that just about beats all! Just what were you up to, anyway?" Theo demanded.

"I'd say about a thousand feet," he said, trying to make light of it, and only making matters worse. He winked at Phoebe.

"Twenty-one hundred, according to the altimeter," Beatrix corrected him.

"Beatrix, would you say I deported myself as a proper gentleman the whole time, and perfectly comfortable without having a chaperone present?"

"Absolutely. And I am sure you would say I behaved as a proper lady," she answered, smiling faintly.

"There, you see, Theo. We didn't even need a chaperone. Everything was on the up and up."

"Horace! This isn't about that, and you know it! It's about taking off to go barn-storming across the country and not telling anyone what you were doing or where you were going. You scared the day-lights out of us. You had Phoebe in tears. You didn't think of that did you? No! Of course not!"

"But Grandfather, did you and Doctor Howell have fun?" Phoebe asked. "Doctor Howell, will you take me up in your plane some day?"

"I would be happy to, but you have to change your name to Josephine, or it won't work," Beatrix answered. Phoebe looked puzzled, and to everyone's surprise Beatrix started singing an old song, "Come Josephine in my flying machine! Up we go! Up we go!"

"And you," Harriet, interrupted, "You stole a painting to take along for your outing. Was that part of your idea of fun? You could have at least told me what you would had in mind."

"You were very busy this morning, and I did not want to interrupt you again. We did not exactly steal it. I believe it was more of a case of borrowing it without first asking," Beatrix said.

"You said it was an old masterpiece. It could have been damaged or blown out of the plane. What were you thinking?" Harriet demanded.

"If you remember correctly, I did not say it was an old masterpiece. I said it looked like an old master, and you told me to curate it. I did, and I assure you it is not old. It was painted in the Italian High Renaissance style, but it is less than fifty years old. To be honest, the frame is worth more than the painting," she said quietly.

"You're saying.....?" Harriet started to ask.

"That the painting is worthless. Yes, that is what I am saying. We took it up to Holland to have it x-rayed. That procedure does no damage of course." Beatrix handed Harriet one of the glass plates. "You can see for yourself, beneath this painting is another one. I believe it is by Schmedilak, who had more artistic aspirations than either talent or technique. In my opinion he is hardly worthy of being called We also looked at some of the paint under a microscope. Even without doing a chemical analysis, it is modern commercial paint. I would not be surprised if it is nothing more than common ordinary house paint."

"If this is someone's idea of a joke, it is a very tasteless one. And if it was a forgery, it's criminal!" Harriet gasped.

"Exactly. As you said, you wanted me to investigate, and I did, along with Horace, of course. Now you know the truth," Beatrix said flatly.

Harriet steadied herself on the back of a chair, her face drained of color.

Horace added, "I think, Harriet, there's a very real possibility that someone has been setting you up for a fall ever since the picture arrived. Humiliation, at the very least. Ruining your career, certainly. The vandalism, the painting. They're all of the same fabric."

"And this is somehow related to the murder?" Theo asked.

"No. I doubt it. Mischief making, even this painting, is small potatoes to taking someone's life. They're two separate stories, with a lot of bad timing. But now, all we have to figure out is who's trying to get you," Horace said.

"I can't imagine who," Harriet said softly. She didn't resist as Phoebe carefully took the painting and the x-ray plate from her mother, then squeezed onto the chair to comfort her.

"My money is on those two or three local ladies," Clarice said.

"You mean Sylvia, Cora, and Louise? No! They're not the type to do that," Harriet objected

"Better make it four. Don't forget that puffed-up old dame who tries to run everything around here. I've been hearing a lot about her," Fred added.

"Mrs. Breckinridge?" Harriet asked. "No, definitely not. I've known all them for years. At Ox-Bow, in town, school, church, everywhere. They're friends. They wouldn't do something like this. And, she certainly does not try to run everything."

"My dear, never underestimate the treachery of another woman, nor a conspiracy between two or more against another. Do so at your peril, that's what my mother told me. Women can be each other's best friends and then turn around and stab them in the back. Trust me dear, I've been through more battles than Theo, Horace, and Fred put together," Clarice said gently.

"I can just see it! Handbags at dawn!" Fred chortled, and was instantly rewarded with fierce glares from everyone in the room. True or not, it was the wrong thing to say at the wrong time.

The damage was done. Harriet collapsed into tears, once again worrying her daughter.

"I'm proud of you for hanging on this long, dear. You're a strong woman. Now, let's the two of us get some fresh air." Clarice said, taking Harriet by the hand. On deck, away from others, she told Harriet, "When I was a young girl I'd always go into the bathroom and run the tap so no one could hear me cry. And then I'd wash my face, put on a bit of rouge, and it was shoulders back and head up, and start again. A good cold water tap does a world of good, and we are surrounded by water. I'm not the only one, either."

Phoebe came out to join them. Clarice paused, and looking down the street said, "Phoebe, your piano teacher is here. The best thing you can do right now to help your mother is to learn how to play the piano. That's going to make her happy."

The girl brightened up. "Oh, and look. So are Mr. Stoddard and Trix and Ollie! Now we can make some REAL music instead of just doing scales!" She fairly skipped off to the lounge.

Harriet and Clarice watched her, envious of how quickly a child could go from tears one minute to joy the next.

"Oh dear. Brace yourself, Harriet. You haven't heard her Mrs. Hansen and Mr. Stoddard squabble. Come on, we'll just let Horace deal with them. It'll serve him right, won't it?" Clarice's suggestion was rewarded with a slight giggle. The two women watched as Beatrix walked out of the library and went down the gangplank.

When the two brothers were finally alone in the library, Theo said, "Look, I'm sorry about blowing up at you, but you had me scared. The idea of something happening to you...." He paused, his lips tightening. "Now look, I think you ought to watch your back around Beatrix. She isn't quite all she says she is. There is something not quite right, and I think she could be more dangerous than you realize."

Theo told his brother about the telephone call with Doctor Sackett. Despite all he said, Horace was still not convinced.

"Look, all she said was that she worked in a lab, and from what you just said, that's what she did. She worked in Sackett's lab, past tense, not that she was still employed there."

"Granted. Fine. Semantics. We assumed too much. But how do you explain these?" Theo asked, holding up two dark bottles labelled Royal Jelly. You, of all people ought to know better than to get mixed up in this sort of quackery. Father fought those snake oil peddlers for years; we did it when we were first starting out, and you know it! So why are you falling for it now? You can't be that gullible!"

"I'm not convinced it is quackery. When I was in London, Conan Doyle and I spent a couple of evenings at his club talking about Royal Jelly. It makes sense to me, and I believe he might be onto something. He's not the only one, either, and I'm willing to take the chance by finding out. There's nothing more to it than that."

"It still worries me. You worry me. You listen to a mystery writer who hasn't seen a patient in decades who thinks he has some fountain of youth, and you fall for it. And now, today, taking off on some fool's errand in an aeroplane with, well, to be honest, someone I still think might be the killer."

"That will do!" Horace exploded in anger. "We'll discuss this later. Right now, let's get back to what's important around here. The mischief has come to an end, but then there is this painting, and a murder. You know what I think? I don't think any of them are related. The vandalism was one thing, done for who knows what reason. We have no idea about the painting, other than that we know it isn't an antique or valuable. That's all we know. Maybe it is nothing more than someone's copy. Maybe it was someone's idea of a joke to send it up here like it was the real item. We don't know. No one knows. And, we won't know until we find out who did it, and that isn't very likely.

"I'm beginning to think that maybe Garrison is right. The murder was a robbery gone wrong. Let's face facts, no one is going to get murdered over a worthless painting."

"Yeah. But there was a murder and the killer hasn't been caught, so let's not let our guard down, just the same. Besides," Theo chuckled, "it'll keep Fred busy. Now, is there any of your prescription medicine left in your cabinet?" Theo asked. Just as they had both done with each other many times in the past, Theo was willing to back off a little. Time would give Horace a chance to think, and they could probably approach it later.

Horace opened the door and pulled out the bottle. "Seems some of it has evaporated. You wouldn't know anything about that, now would you?" Horace asked.

"Who me? Well, you know how it is. You and Beatrix suddenly go missing, and then I found those pills. I figured I should check your medicine just to be sure it was all right," Theo teased.

"And?"

"Well, it seemed to be allright. But I think a second opinion might be a good idea." Theo said as he raised his glass. Both men relaxed, knowing that their squabble was over for the moment.

"There was something else strange about the painting. I didn't tell you earlier," Horace said. "A lab tech noticed that on the bottom of the frame, where you could barely see it, were the letters D U X. Any idea what that could mean?"

"Probably nothing more than the initials of the carpenter who made it. It's a bit odd, though. I've seen those letters before somewhere, but I can't remember where."

Harriet came to the study door, putting a finger over her lips. "Listen," she whispered. From the lounge they could hear the piano being played.

"Phoebe?" Horace whispered.

"No. It's your friends from the band. They were up here a few minutes ago, and Mr. Stoddard asked Mrs. Hansen if he could play an old song for her. Would you believe it, she agreed? She not only let him play it, but she liked it, and asked him to play it again. He did, and then she picked it up right away."

"What was the song?"Horace asked. "Something by one of her long-lost long-haired ancestors?"

"No. It's a new piece by Irving Berlin. A song called 'What'll I Do?' And get this, the other two, Trix and Ollie, just asked Mrs. Hansen to play it on stage tonight at the Big Pavilion, and she said she would. She played it again, and Mr. Stoddard said she played better than he did. So, she agreed to play it as a solo."

"And just how is this good news?" Theo asked. "Aside from a bit of peace and quiet for a change?"

"He's won her over. Maybe she won't be so nasty and they won't be at each other's throats all the time," Harriet explained.

"Even five minutes would be a welcome relief!" Horace added.

"Well, Ollie gave us tickets for tonight. After all we've been through, I think we need a break – we ARE going," Harriet announced.

DEATH BY PALLET KNIFE

CHAPTER TWELVE

Mrs. Garwood prepared a light dinner for them, and at Harriet's suggestion and despite her protects and objections, everyone pitched in to clear the table and put things away in the galley. "All right everyone, twenty minutes to get ready for our night out!" Horace announced when the work was done. "Twenty minutes, not twenty-one."

"And to be on time we have to be ten minutes early, right Grandfather? You always say that!" she rolled her eyes to tease him, then skipped off to her cabin to freshen up.

"Good girl. You're learning!"

Precisely on the mark, Fred snapped to attention and saluted Doctor Horace. "All present and accounted for, Sir! Volunteering to take the point, Sir!"

Horace was nonplussed by his driver's sudden burst of military formality and merely muttered, "Carry on," shaking his head in amusement as Fred did an about-face and shouted, "Forward".

They made a grand procession down Water Street towards the Big Pavilion, with Fred leading the way and Theo and Clarice behind him. Like his brother, Theo was wearing his straw boater, and Clarice was in a dress far longer than the latest fashion. When Theo mentioned the length, she had said icily her legs didn't warrant looking like a flapper. He just laughed and asked, "Says who?" The Garwoods followed, just in front of Harriet and Phoebe. For a few yards Horace and Beatrix walked next to each other at a wide distance, but then she shot ahead to change places with Phoebe.

" Grandfather, everyone is looking at us like we're movie stars!" Phoebe said in awe. Feeling very grown up, she took his arm the way she had seen other women walk with a man. Horace said nothing, but did doff his hat when someone called his name.

"How come you're not using your silver-headed cane tonight?" she asked.

"Oh, didn't think I'd need it, so I took this one. And, it's a walking stick, not a cane. Besides, I'm escorting my girl, so I don't need one."

"I'll remember," she promised with a long sigh, proud that he thought so highly of her.

Their seats were near the front and to the right of the main stage, and while they waited for the show to start, they sipped at their lemonade, talking steadily louder as the seats filled and the noise level steadily increased, and they tried to hear one another over the conversations of the others. Horace watched as Fred got up to go over to talk to a man near the edge of the crowd. A few minutes later he returned with a coffee cup.

"That'll keep you up all night," Horace warned him.

"I thought you might like to try something different," he said, slightly nodding his head and looking down at the cup. He handed it to his boss. Horace took a very small sip, paused for a moment, then whispered to Fred, "What is it?"

"It's mead. Honey mead, some call it. Honey wine. Same stuff that the girl out to Ox-Bow gave you. I wouldn't drink too much of it if I were you, which I'm not. It has a way of catching up with a man unexpectedly."

"Where'd you get it?"

Fred nodded in the general direction of the man he had just seen. "Remember me telling you about a fellow they were calling Red out to Mrs. Hansen's place? That's him over there. I heard tell that he's in with some of the fellows in Chicago, but no one talks much about him around here."

"It goes down smooth," Horace said.

"That's the general idea. A fellow gets a couple of rounds for his girl on account of the fact that it doesn't burn like that homemade hooch, and....."

"I get the idea, Fred, that's enough with the ladies here."

"Now, if you want me to do it, I can get a coffee cup for the Ice Queen," Fred whispered as he tipped his head slightly in Beatrix's direction. "Might defrost her a little."

"Absolutely not! So our piano teacher is a bootlegger," he laughed. "That beats all."

"Sure does."

"And, it looks like she runs her own distribution out at the school," Horace added, remembering the flask Pauline had given him. "Now, take this stuff and go water a plant with it."

"You sure."

"Positive. Now, go, and don't bring any more of it around here. But listen, if you just happen to find a couple of bottles of it, you know, that fall of that truck you're always talking about, you be sure to bring them into my library," Horace said with a wink. "Just for safe keeping."

Horace was lost in thought. If Mrs. Hansen was making and selling honey wine, maybe the professor had gotten wind of what she was doing. And maybe he wasn't a professor at all, but an undercover agent. She had access to knives, and a personality that kept people at arm's length, only maybe he got too close. And maybe she was the one doing the mischief. The only thing was, she didn't seem to be the type to know much about art. Then again....."

He was interrupted by Phoebe. "Grandfather! There's Trix! And there's Mr Stoddard! It's starting!" she tugged at his sleeve. The crowd started applauding, and a few rowdies in the rear starting clapping in unison, hoping to get the others to join them.

Ollie Anderson came to the front of the stage, holding an old-fashioned megaphone in one hand. He held up his hands to quiet the audience, then gave a welcome and announced at the end of the first set they were going to have a real treat – a local musician making her professional debut. "SOOOOO, folks, sit and enjoy the music, or come down to the dance floor. Our first piece is one you all know. Paul Whiteman introduced it a few years, and it's still popular: 'The Charleston!'" Several younger couples hurried to dance, and to Horace's amusement, Theo led Clarice out to the floor. They weren't doing the latest steps, but then, neither were some other couples. Theo was smooth with the Fox trot, and Horace winced that he didn't have his ability to dance. Even if he couldn't admit it out loud, he was too inhibited.

To their surprise, the caretaker from the school stopped by their table, spruced up, with his black hair slicked back. At first it looked like John Reynolds was going to ask Harriet for a dance, but then thought better of it. The two of them talked for a few minutes before he moved on.

Horace felt he had to do something. It was awkward, sitting there next to Beatrix, not speaking, not even knowiing what to say. He knew he should be polite and ask her to dance, but he couldn't dance, and he knew it. She beat him to it: "You don't Charleston, do you Horace?" Beatrix asked firmly.

"Not really," he said.

She gave him a wintry smile, relieved. So was Horace.

The Charleston was followed by the "The Varsity Rag," "The Bearcat somp" and the "Indiana Shuffle" before Ollie came back to the front of his band.

"I'm happy to see you all enjoying yourselves. Now, you won't want to dance to this one. Now, I promised earlier we had a real treat in store for you tonight. I think everyone knows Mister Irvin Berlin's "What'll I Do?", and we've got our own version of it for you tonight. Now folks, if it doesn't turn out right, well then, just consider it our own rendering of it. On piano is Lloyd Stoddard, but right now he's going to sit this one out, at least at first. Taking his place is Saugatuck's very own Roletta Hansen, better known to some of you as Fredericka Chopin, is going to start this one off. Fellows, when Lloyd makes it a four-handed piece, join in and take it from there. We're not dancing, but folks, if you know this love-song, sing along!

The locals in the crowd were stunned at first, certain it was some sort of a gag, but then wildly applauding and whistling as she came on stage and took a bow. She was stiff and uncomfortable until she sat down on the piano bench. Softly, almost tentatively at first, she played the song. She did it a second time, this time much louder, then nodded toward Lloyd to join her. The two of them sat side by side as they played it through.

Suddenly, from the rear of the band, Ollie cut loose with the drums, playing a long riff to change the tempo. Trix stood up with his trombone and began playing. Three clarinets and two saxo-phones joined them, and finally the muted trumpets. Lloyd mo-tioned with his left hand to pick up the pace, with Roletta keeping up with him. "Hope your corset isn't too tight, girl! Theme and variation, theme and variation, and here we go with the variations!"

He broke into a big smile, flawlessly converting a ballad into a driving jazz piece.

The home town folks were stunned. It seemed impossible that Roletta would ever lower her standards to so much as come into the Big Pavilion, much less play on stage, and jazz, at that. They loved it, and loved it all the more because they could see Roletta was having fun. Ollie pounded out a staccato on the snares, the band's signal to bring it to an end.

The crowd was on their feet, applauding, whistling, and demanding another tune. It started near the back, "More! More! More!" until the chant filled the room.

"Well, you heard your fans, Roletta," Ollie said. "You want to do another one?"

"Another one? I got plenty where that came from! You fellows know Jelly Roll Morton's "Tin Roof Blues? Let's do it!"

"You play it, and we'll catch up with you," Ollie told her through the megaphone.

Her hands covered the entire keyboard as she started, flying over the keys in the 'Glide Style'. Half way through, it was the banjo player who caught the key and started strumming. The woods joined, and then the brass. All of them started passing the tune between them, then quieted down, certain that it would come to an end. Instead, she called out, "Who's Sorry Now?" She pounded he left foot on the floor to set the tempo. She nodded to Ollie, and he smiled back in return. She'd do another piece.

Three jazz pieces, one after another! Harriet and Phoebe were stunned. There had never been such a show in the history of the Big Pavilion. Even Lloyd was surprised by her. "Guess you're all right after all, little sister," he said, shaking his head in amazement. "I didn't know you had it in you. Sure didn't see that one coming!"

Ollie had to think fast to regain control of his show. "Who's Sorry Now?" Well, if you ask me, it's anyone who didn't hear our guest pianist is going to be sorry come tomorrow morning!" The crowd roared; the noise so deafening that both Horace and Beatrix were winching in pain. "Okay folks, we're going to give you a chance to catch your breath, have some refreshments, and we'll be back on stage in about fifteen minutes."

As the musicians were leaving the stage, Theo glanced over at Beatrix. She was sitting ram rod straight, staring straight ahead, her face ashen, almost as if she was going into shock. "Are you alright?" he asked. "Perhaps some fresh air?" It was all she could do to nod her head. She didn't move. "Why don't we go outside for a few minutes during the break?" he suggested. She didn't move, and he reached over to touch her right hand that was resting on the table. It caught her attention and made her flinch. "Shall we go outside?" he asked yet again. Wordlessly, she followed him out the door, her arms folded tightly across her chest.

Beatrix inhaled deeply, as the color started to come back to her face. "It was a bit loud," Theo said quietly and gently.

"Yes."

The two of them stood under a massive oak tree, silent, waiting for the other to speak.

"And the crowd made it feel confining. Noise, a big crowd, and I do not get along," she said, her eyes focused on the dunes on other side of the river. "Yes, loud. I am better now. Please, do not let me keep you from the others."

"I'll wait with you. It gives me a chance to ask you about this Royal Jelly medicine you prescribed for Horace."

She turned and looked at him. "What has he told you?"

"Not much, which is usual for Horace, other than he claims it helps him focus more, well, ever since getting out of the hospital, that is. He keeps his cards close to his chest. Did he ever tell you why he ended up in the hospital and what happened?"

"Yes," she said.

"And.....?"

Beatrix looked at Theo, debating whether to share his brother's confidences. "I believe you will be relieved to know there is nothing wrong with Horace other than he made a mistake forgetting to look both ways before crossing the street, and he got brushed back by a car. A taxi, I believe. A few bruises, maybe some stretched tendons and muscles. There was no physical damage."

"But.....?"

"But, he realized he looked right rather than left, and that troubled him. He obsessively believed, his mind is beginning to weaken," she said softly.

"But there is nothing wrong with his mind or his memory," Theo objected.

"Yes, I agree. His mind is very sharp for a man half his age. You know that and I know that. He could not accept it. The Royal Jelly I gave him is nothing more than capsules of honey. Horace is now convinced they are working, and I think you can see a difference in his general disposition, can you not?"

Theo's mouth was open but the words were not coming out.

"In other words, I gave him a harmless placebo. Harmless."

Theo was still trying to find the right words. He finally murmured, "Thank you. I'll keep your secret."

The two stood under the tree for a while, and watched as Clarice and her daughter, and Horace came out, looked around, and walked toward them.

"A bit too loud in there for me," Horace said. "I've had enough and am going home."

"And I know one young lady who has stayed up far too late – again," Harriet said. "Horace, as long as you are....?"

"Of course."

"If you do not mind, I would like to walk along back to the boat with you. I believe I have had sufficient entertainment for one night," Beatrix said.

"Are you sure you want to leave so early, Beatrix?" Harriet asked.

"Yes. I think that was enough for me," she said firmly. "It was more than enough. I'm ready to leave."

"Well, Phoebe," her grandfather said, holding out to his hand to her, "looks to me like I get to escort two girls home."

"I promise, I won't be long," Harriet said, giving her daughter a kiss on the forehead, then asking Horace," You're sure it won't be a problem?"

"Not at all," he answered.

"Do I get a bedtime story, Grandfather?" she asked.

"Well, which one do you want?"

He was expecting a request for Beatrix Potter or Milne's *Winnie the Pooh*, perhaps another chapter or two of *The Wizard of Oz*. Instead, she squeezed his hand and asked, "Would you read me *The Hound of the Baskervilles*?"

"No! It's far too long and not the sort of thing a young lady should read unless she wants nightmares. We'll save that for another time. And, in the daylight!"

"Well, Doctor Howell, do you have a favourite Sherlock Holmes story?" the girl asked.

"Yes, Yes, I do," she said brightly. "My favourite is *A Scandal in Bohemia*. I read it when I was just a bit older than your age, many years ago. Irene Adler was a hero to me. Maybe you'll think so, too." She looked over Phoebe's head and practically winked at Horace. Whatever had troubled his childhood friend earlier that evening had apparently dissipated.

"Then Sherlock Holmes and Irene Adler it is tonight!" Horace said.

When they got to the *Aurora* Beatrix excused herself, promising to join them in a few minutes. "Don't wait for me. I already know the story," she said as she went down the hall, then turned around and added, "Practically by heart."

Horace opened the door to his study and froze.

CHAPTER THIRTEEN

"I was hoping you'd be staying longer at the Big Pavilion. Now, close the door! Keep your hands where I can see them. Just stay still and keep quiet."

Horace and Phoebe were staring at John Reynolds, sitting behind the desk, looking down the barrel of Horace's pistol in his right hand.

"Thoughtful of you to leave it in the drawer," he smirked, waving it at them.

"I think you need to explain yourself. What's the idea of coming on to my boat without permission and breaking into my office like this?" Horace told him, pushing Phoebe behind him. His voice was surprisingly calm.

"You and your lady friend were getting a bit too close. That makes me jumpy. I don't like it when people get in the way, especially in my way. I broke in to see if you had written any notes or anything. The desk was the best place to look, and instead, I found your pistol."

"I'm not following you," Horace said.

"You're too curious, and you know what they say about curious cats. They get killed."

"You're intending to shoot me?" Horace asked.

"If it comes to that, I won't hesitate. I ought to, just on principle. You messed up my plans and got in my way. You ruined everything. So, yeah, maybe I will. You'll deserve it if I do."

"And just what did I do? Mind telling me?"

Reynolds snickered. "Come on, old timer, you can figure it out all on your own. Like I said, you got in my way."

"I'm still not following you. Why don't you explain it?" Horace asked quietly. The two men continued to stare at each other, neither of them daring to move.

"Grandfather, would you like your silver headed cane while you're standing? Would you?" Phoebe asked.

"Yes, why, yes I would Phoebe." He told her, making certain not to let a tell-tale smile slip across his face. He hoped he understood why she phrases her question so oddly.

He reached a hand behind him to take it, keeping his eyes on Reynolds all the time, making a twisting motion with his hand once he grasped it. He could feel Phoebe helping to unscrew it. "Yes, Reynolds, I do want to know. You'd better explain it to me," he said firmly.

The two men glared at each other, saying nothing.

At that moment Beatrix came through the door. For a second Reynolds was distracted by the movement, and took his eyes off of Horace. Phoebe held tightly on the staff of his walking stiff while Horace pulled out the blade, the steel flashing in the air, and firmly pressed the tip of the sword against the left side of Reynold's neck. He pressed it enough to make him wince.

Beatrix gasped and swallowed hard, recovering quickly. "I seem to be interrupting a private conversation. My apologies. I will leave," she said quietly. "Phoebe, come along with me, now."

Reynolds laughed. "Oh no you don't, girlie. You're not going anywhere. You're the other one I want to settle a score with. The two of you are in cahoots. Just come in and move over here where I can see you. And close that door behind you. Sword or no sword, I'll plug you if that girl tries to get away."

Beatrix did as she was told, moving to the side of the desk. The two men remained locked in a death stare.

Horace took the initiative. "You've had your chance, Reynolds, and you didn't want to talk. Now, it's my turn, and I suggest you listen very carefully if you want to live. That's an old double action Colt, and you haven't cocked it yet. You may think I've slowed down, but I swear, if your thumb so much as twitches, if you try cocking it, this blade goes into your carotid artery. If I slice the artery, the pain will be horrible at first while I cut through nerve endings, but it won't last long. Normally, you would be given anaesthesia to deaden the nerve endings. Not this time. Instead, you'll watch your life's blood spurting up to the ceiling and down the walls. A lot of it, all of it, in fact. You'll go into shock and then your heart will stop, and it will make a mess of my library, but right now, I don't give two raps in Hades about that. And you'd better trust me on this, when a man sees himself bleeding to death, he doesn't want to think about anything else. Understand?"

"Nice talk, old man, but you're not the only one who's been in combat and seen men die. I'll take my chances."

Horace pushed the blade tighter against his neck. "Put the gun down. Now."

"Drop your sword If I pull the trigger it'll knock you against the wall before you can cut me."

"You forgot to notice that I'm leaning over the desk. Leaning into you. How much do you know about physics? You won't have time to move away. It's an old gun. It takes a lot of effort to pull the hammer back, and to pull the trigger. That gives me plenty of time to slit the artery. You might shoot me, but you'll still be dead. I promise."

"Go to hell, old man!"

Horace didn't let Reynolds rattle him, but remained steady, his speech measured. "Now, you tell me something before I send you there first. Did you kill that man out on the meadow?"

Reynolds chuckled. "Figure that one out on your own, old man, or did your lady friend here have to explain it to you?"

"And, you did it with a serrated combat knife or bayonet, didn't you?" Beatrix asked.

That was a question that startled him, all the more so since it came from a woman. "Yeah. That's right. How'd you get lucky to guess that?" He snorted in derision. "Surprised a girlie like you would know about it."

"It is not a matter of luck. It is observation and deduction. Because you are old enough to have been in the war. You are right handed, and yet the fourth finger on your left hand is missing."

"Yeah, so what? I got wounded."

"No. No you did not. I believe it was intentional, not a wound."

"How you figure that one, lady?"

"It is quite simple, really. I will explain what you already know. You are holding the pistol in your right hand, and you were a soldier. Probably you were in the infantry, and you lost one finger. Just one. The fourth finger on a person's left hand is almost useless because the tendons are weak there. The tendons and muscles are so weak that the finger rarely works very well independently unless it is on a piano, organ, or typewriter. It's the only finger truly expendable.

"Here is what I think happened: you were out on picket duty one night, scared, maybe a little shell-shocked and frightened that you were not going to live to see the next dawn. So, you took the coward's way out. You lit a cigarette and tied it to your fourth finger.

You crouched down in the trench, holding up your hand, counting on a sniper to aim at it. A nice little war wound that would get you sent home while your comrades fought and died. And no one would ever suspect you of cowardice.

"As for why I know you used a bayonet. You would have used it in hand to hand combat. For what the reason, you serrated your blade. Perhaps you are a sadist and did it to inflict more pain. You knew that if you were captured with it you would be executed on the spot. Your own officers should have ordered summary execution. It is against international law. But like most cowards you put on a brave front. You wanted to show your buddies just how tough you were and how you were fearless in front of the Hun. So, you notched your bayonet and boasted about it. Tell me, am I right?" Beatrix asked.

"Close. Almost. But they were Austrians and Bulgarians, not Germans. I was on the Italian front. Mountain division. And yeah, I liked sticking them with a bayonet. I liked the look in their eyes just before I did it." He cackled out a laugh. "You should have seen the look on those Bulgars just before they got it. I did my duty, and I deserved to get sent home. And now you're going to get what you deserve."

"Good work, Sherlock," Horace told Beatrix. He was truly impressed.

"Irene," Beatrix corrected him. "Irene Adler, if you please."

The two men stared at each other, waiting for the other to make the first move. Beatrix's eyes darted between them, and toward where Phoebe was crouching behind Horace.

"You two are having what I believe is called by some people as a Mexican Stand-off," Beatrix sighed. "Horace, would you mind if I had one of your cigars while we work this out?"

"By all means. Reynolds, would you care for one?" Horace taunted him. "Go ahead. Take your pick"

"You must take me for a real patsy, old-timer, thinking I'd fall for a trick like that!"

Beatrix took a cigar out of the box, and to Horace's surprise, in a most unladylike move, bit off the end and spit it on the floor at Reynolds' feet.

"And Horace, would you mind if I used your new lighter? Would that be alright?"

"Please do. You know how it works." He told her. To Reynolds, he added. "Don't worry. You're either going to put your gun down or I'm going to do surgery on your neck. But I have better sense than to let Doctor Howell blow us all to smithereens with a grenade. It's a novelty lighter. My man Fred got it for me. You probably saw him out at the school."

Beatrix held the cigar to the left side of her mouth, pulled hard on the pin and let it slip out of her fingers onto the floor. She dropped the cigar and cried, "It didn't light! Horace, it didn't light!"

"All right. Put the pin back in, and keep holding on to the lever. Squeeze tight and don't let go. Where's the pin?"

"I don't know. It's on the floor somewhere. Horace, this isn't a lighter. It's a live grenade!"

Almost in unison Horace and Reynolds shouted, "Don't let go of the handle!"

Beatrix was panting in fear, and Horace hoped she would drop down to the floor, distract Reynolds, maybe even shove him out of the way, so Horace could get the gun out of his hand. She didn't move.

Horace used the distraction to push Phoebe closer to the door. She understood, and reached behind her back for the knob, grabbed and turned it. The door made a slight noise, but Beatrix was shouting she couldn't find the pin.

"Get that thing out of here, woman! Toss it in the river and get back in here. Remember, I got your boyfriend in my sights. Do it, woman! Do it now! Now!"

Beatrix held the grenade at arm's length, staring at it, as she backed away towards the door. She took a deep breath, very calmly saying, "Open the door for me, Phoebe." She backed up through the doorway and in a flurry of motion threw the grenade into the far corner of the library, pushed Phoebe out the door hard enough to send her sprawling onto the deck, and pulled Horace by the back of his coat out the door with her. Somehow he managed to switch off the lights to leave Reynolds in the dark. She slammed it shut behind her.

"Brace the door! Quick. Get that deck chair!" Horace told Beatrix. Then he shouted at his granddaughter, "Run. Get help! Now girl!"

Together, Horace and Beatrix pushed the chair under the door know, jamming it shut. "Get down. Get away from the door!" The two of them scrambled across the deck, moving to one side of the boat to get out of the way of the door.

"Let me out of here! Open the door!" Reynolds shouted, throwing himself against it. It didn't budge. In rapid succession he fired off five shots, each of them puncturing the wood and ripping it. All the time, he was screaming in fear that the grenade would go off.

The two of them were panting, their backs against the railing. Finally, they exhaled deeply and smiled. "Well done, Irene," Horace said.

"Well done, Sherlock. And Toby has run to fetch Lestrade," Beatrix laughed nervously between breaths.

"Toby was the dog. I think you mean, Watson."

"Watson, then," Beatrix corrected herself. "Horace," she gasped, "There were only five shots. He's got one left."

"No he doesn't. The fool didn't check the revolver. Never put a bullet in the first chamber. It's the fastest way to shoot yourself in the foot. Or anywhere else, for that matter. Wyatt Earp told me that himself." He reached in his pocket to take out a key ring and handed it to her. "You want the honours? Big skeleton key." Reynolds was pounding on the door and screaming.

Beatrix quickly locked the door and rejoined Horace on the deck.

"You sure do know how to show a lady a good time, Doctor Horace Balfour."

"Just returning the favour from you scaring me to death in your flying machine."

"Oh, I am going to be very sick." Beatrix stood up, holding her hand over her mouth and raced to lean over the rail.

The shots had drawn a crowd, and it was rapidly growing as people hurried out of the Big Pavilion. One young man, perhaps with his confidence bolstered by Mrs. Hansen's honey wine, charged up the gangplank. "You folks alright?" he asked.

Horace stood up, handing Beatrix the pocket square from his jacket so she could attend to her face, told him. "We're fine. There's a madman locked in the library with a gun and a grenade."

"Grenade!" the man turned and bolted back down the gangplank. "Grenade! Grenade! Get back, Everyone! Get back! Grenade!" The crowd pushed back against the curious spectators who were still arriving. A few minutes later, they were pushing up against each other again, this time to make room for Chief Garrison's squad car. Theo was in the front seat. Harriet and Clarice, with Phoebe between them, were in the back. When the chief jumped out with his gun drawn, the crowd gasped.

"What's going on?" he demanded.

"You all right Horace? Beatrix?" Theo asked.

"We're fine. All three of us are fine. Captain, you'll find your murderer inside the library. I suspect he'll be trying to make a run for it. For some reason he thinks there is a live grenade in there with him, about to go off any second." Horace handed the chief the key to the door.

"A grenade? You joshing me?" Garrison asked.

"Well, it looks like a grenade, but it's a cigar lighter. Some army buddies gave it to me. Would you mind giving it to me when you have a chance? I'd like it back, and Beatrix never got to light her cigar." The chief turned to look at him, shaking his head at Doctor Balfour's concern over a cigar.

His gun drawn, Garrison stepped over to the door. "All right. I'm going to unlock and open this door. You'd better be down on your hands and knees or I'll shoot you before you can say Jack Robertson. That clear?"

Beatrix leaned toward Horace, "I believe he should have said 'Jack Robinson.' Horace ignored her.

"Yes, just let me out before it blows up! Anything! Just get me out of here!" When the chief threw open the door, Reynolds crawled forward until Garrison ordered him to stop. "Put the bracelets on. Left hand first, then right." Reynolds obeyed, and was ordered to his feet. "Let's go!"

Garrison and his prisoner paused near where Horace and Beatrix were standing. "I got a lot of questions for you two, but you can tell me now. How did you capture him?"

"Well, the truth of the matter is, he got the drop on me, and then my granddaughter and Doctor Howell out-flanked him," Horace replied.

"With a grenade?"Garrison asked.

"With a grenade," Beatrix answered with a faint smile. "Oh, and your sword cane. That wouldn't be the one Bat Masterson gave you?" she asked.

"I'll never tell," Horace said.

Beatrix gasped and made a second dash toward the railing, this time on the river side.

The police chief squinted at them, wanting to know more. He opened and closed his mind, then shook his head, and said, "I'll tell your chauffeur to drive you down to the station."

There was a faint pink tinge to the eastern sky, and a few birds starting to wake up when Beatrix and Horace finished at the police station. Garrison didn't offer them a ride home, and Horace had sent Fred back to the boat hours earlier. "It's only a couple of blocks," Horace observed. "Walk?"

"I hope we don't wake anyone up when we get there," Beatrix yawned.

"Knowing my family, we won't be that lucky. They'll probably all be waiting up for us."

At the foot of the gangplank Beatrix turned to him. "You never told me what you do to keep your mind active now that you are retired. When you are not taking on Chicago mobsters and psychotic killers, that is."

"Oh, you know, just the usual stuff old duffers do. Slaying dragons, pouring hot oil down from the top of the castle walls to keep the barbarians at bay, rescuing damsels in distress," he teased, punch-drunk from a lack of sleep.

"This must be a change, being rescued by a damsel," she teased back.

"Two damsels."

She snorted in laughter. "Two."

They started up the gangplank and paused to look at the library door. Harriet said quietly, "Your boat got shot up. I am sorry. Can it be repaired?"

"That seems to go with the territory every time I come to Saugatuck. Well, let's face the welcoming committee. They've all waited up for us.

"Grandfather!" Phoebe shrieked with joy, running across the lounge to give him a hug. She took his hand and led him to his favourite leather chair.

"Well, did he confess?" Theo asked.

"As our colourful friends in Chicago would say, 'he sung like a canary'. Confessed to everything. I doubt we'll even have to stay for the trial."

"What I want to know is how you figured out it was John Reynolds," Harriet asked once they were all seated.

"And lured him into your study?" Clarice asked.

"I didn't. We didn't, that is. None of us. And, to begin with, his name isn't John Reynolds. It's Giovanni Renaldi. His family came over from a village just outside of Naples when he was a youngster, and they changed their name to make it sound more America. The long and short of it is, he grew up in squalor in New York City, and decided he wanted to be a painter."

"Tough choice for a kid in the tenements," Clarice said.

"Well, tough or not, he went back to Italy, to Florence, to study at the academy just before the war broke out. And since he was using his original name again and spoke Italian, he was conscripted into the army and sent to fight the Bulgarians. Let's just say he wasn't much of a soldier. A bully, a sadistic killer, and then he cracked up. Shell shock. He told us as much earlier, and stuck to the story when Garrison grilled him.

"Anyway, after the war he tried to get into the Academy, but they wouldn't have him. I suspect he wasn't qualified, just not good enough to get admitted. Or, maybe they realized he was too un-disciplined. Anyway, they didn't take him, so to make ends meet, he started working on his own and selling them on the street and in the bars. Eventually he got into a couple of small galleries, and somehow scraped together enough money to get back to the States. A few years later he ended up in Chicago where he tried to get into the painting school...."

"The School of the Art Institute of Chicago," Harriet interrupted.

"Correct. He didn't have any better luck there than in Florence, but someone gave him a job as a guard at the museum. He didn't say much about it, but I have the idea he saw a notice that Ox-Bow needed a handyman, so he came up here. Maybe he got someone to pull some strings. Who knows?"

Phoebe yawned and then came over to sit on her grandfather's lap, resting her head on his chest, desperately trying to stay awake.

"My belief," Beatrix said, "is that while he was a guard watching over the paintings, he must have decided he could paint in the style of the Italian High Renaissance. Then, when he got here this spring and found out you had been made the temporary director, he thought he deserved the job. Jealousy, envy, arrogance, and without any real qualifications. She said with a shrug. "I believe the painting was to show he was a wonderful artist, or something like that."

Harriet snorted. "To tell you the truth, I wish he had been given the job instead of me. My life would have been much easier this summer."

Beatrix continued, "So, all of that mischief, the vandalism, was to force you out before Mr Fursman or Mr Tallmage returned home. He hated you with a passion and tried to make your life miserable. The vandalism was to be death by a thousand cuts, until you gave up. As for the painting that he claimed he discovered, as I said, it was his work. His mistake was not getting the right type of paint. I suspect he mixed cobalt into some of the pigments to speed up the drying, then baked it in an oven to crack the paint. It is only a guess because I did not have a laboratory to do a chemical analysis. Nor, the time."

"It'd be a hoot if he baked it in that old battlewagon's oven, wouldn't it!" Fred joked.

"But how could you tell? What gave it away?"Clarice asked.

"Horace kept pointing out that there was something odd about the painting, but I did not see it at first. Then, I realized it was right in front of me the entire time. For one thing, the size didn't seem quite right. It was smaller than many paintings from that era. And then for another, the paint was cracked to make it look old, but the painting as a whole was too clean. If the painting was several hundred years old, it should have been much darker from candle smoke and dirt. I should have seen it right from the start. If I had, none of this would have happened," Beatrix moaned.

"But why the murder? Why would someone murder someone over a worthless painting?" Clarice asked.

"Harriet, Mr. Reynolds had time off from work, did he not?"

"Well yes. Every other week from Friday afternoon to Monday noon," Harriet said slowly. "Why? Why would that be important?"

"Chief Garrison found some train ticket stubs in his pockets. Reynolds confessed that he took the train into the city on his free days. He said he went to the museum to study old paintings, sketch, and read about them in the library. Somehow he must have heard or learned that Professor Pulchini from the Academy in Florence was visiting. And remember, they had a long history. Pulchini was on the admissions committee and interview Reynolds. Reynolds blamed him for being turned down.

"But surely, after all this time Pulchini wouldn't have remembered him," Harriet objected.

"No, probably not. But Reynolds would have remembered him, and that is what mattered He was afraid Pulchini would have asked questions, or told someone here – you, Harriet – about his past failure. He could not abide that. So, when Reynolds saw him, he could not take any chances. And..."

"So he killed him in cold blood," Harriet said. "That is such a waste of life."

"But that still doesn't explain the palette knife," Theo objected.

"No. No it does not. Certainly, it would not be something a rational man would do. But the man is insane. Criminally insane. He killed Pulchini to protect himself, and then put the palette knife in the wound as a symbol of revenge. Frankly, if he hadn't used the palette knife, he might have gotten away with it, and Garrison would have his unsolvable robbery and murder," Beatrix said.

"Or....." Horace looked firmly at his daughter-in-law until she drew in her breath in sock.

"Or, I might have been next. Is that what you're saying?"

"Yes," Horace said softly. "Very likely. He was mentally disintegrating. He'd killed many times during the war, some of them sadistically so. And, he'd just tasted blood again. Once you do one murder, it isn't so difficult to do it again. "

"It is also very probable that he would have become paranoid and believed that you knew he was guilty," Beatrix told them.

Phoebe suddenly got up sudden and crossed the room to hug tightly to her mother when she heard her gasp.

"I would have been next, Reynolds would have volunteered to take over, and then reveal the painting and expected to be acclaimed as a great artist. Oh, that man, that poor man, to be so deluded."

"All right, all right. Now, I want to know how you knew the grenade was a dud," Theo said. "You two were taking a big chance."

Beatrix flashed Theo a quick smile. "Not at all. Fred told me that he had given it to Horace, and Horace said the same thing, and showed me how it worked. I knew all along. Fortunately, Reynolds did not."

"And then we played your game!" Phoebe said suddenly.

"Game? What game? What's the girl talking about?" Theo demanded.

"Beatrix told me about the word game she and Grandfather invented when they were my age, and how you never caught on to it. They would ask each other a question with a code word at the beginning to get the right answer. That's why you thought they could read each other's minds," Phoebe said with triumph.

"I don't remember any game like that. And, I certainly don't remember thinking you could read minds, Horace. Half the time it seemed as if you were somewhere else, with your nose in a book wrapped away in your own little world," Theo growled. "Phoebe, you'll have to explain it."

"Well, the game belongs to a very top-secret club, so I shouldn't give away the secrets. Would you say that is right, Grandfather?"

"That's right. You wouldn't disagree with that, Harriet?"

"No." Her lips tightened to hide a smile.

"I haven't the slightest idea what you two are going on about," Harriet said.

"There's a bit more about our Mr. Reynolds. He was more deluded than you realize. There's a new government in Italy. Well, it's not all that new, but it's run by Mussolini, and he's always ranting and chest pounding about the grandeurs of ancient Rome, and how he wants to build up the old empire. Reynolds said he wanted to go back to Italy with his paintings, and become a painter for Il Duce," Horace said. "As I said, the man cracked up. He's insane."

"Il Duce? Wait a minute. Wait just a minute. The other day you said something about some letters on the bottom inside of the frame...."

"Stretcher," Beatrix said.

"Frame, stretcher. Fine. Some letters. 'D U X' you said, and I said I'd seen them before." Theo stood up and sorted through some cards in his wallet. "Here. Here it is. From that consulate Priori." He handed Horace the card. "See, down at the bottom – D U X . It has something to do with the government."

"DUX means Mussolini," Fred said. "Boss, we saw that when we were in Rome. They had those letters all over the place."

"So, he did this in honour of Mussolini, hoping to curry favour with him," Harriet said slowly.

"As I said, he's insane," Horace repeated.

CHAPTER FOURTEEN

Over breakfast four days later, Beatrix announced that she was returning home. The abruptness of her announcement startled everyone, especially Theo and Clarice. She gave a faint smile, and once again looking passed them, explained that the police chief had given her permission to leave. "It is time to go. I am getting jumpy being away, and I have work to do."

"Back to work at Sackett's laboratory?" Theo asked.

"No, I was forced to retire a couple of years ago because of my age. It was very much against my will, but they said they had a policy of making room for younger pathologists."

"So, just what do you do?" Theo asked.

"I am still a pathologist, only now I work as a consultant for museums, galleries, and private collectors. In reality, it is much the same type of work, and it utilizes my background in chemistry and art history."

"Don't you miss the laboratory and working with other people?" Clarice asked.

"No. Once I left, I do not think I ever thought about it. Anyway, this has been a unique experience and far more adventurous than most of my work. I have already packed, and I hope it would not be imposing if you gave me a ride out to my aeroplane, Fred."

"Do I get to turn the propeller again?" he asked with a smile.

"Yes, I would be grateful."

"We'll all go," Horace said. "We'll see you off properly."

Beatrix paused and looked at him. "I do not think anyone has ever seen me off before. Many times I wonder if they are more comfortable when I leave."

"We're not that way. I think we all wish you would stay," Horace said.

Beatrix shook her head. "No. I must leave."

Well, first time solving a murder; first time having a farewell committee," Horace said, without much enthusiasm in his voice. "Fred, you'd better find a taxi so we can all go."

The two cars drove to the edge of the grassy field, all of them saying their good-byes at a safe distance. Just as when she had arrived, Phoebe helped with her flying bag as the two of them walked across the grass. Fred trailed behind to help start the engine.

"Horace, go out and say goodbye to her properly," Harriet told him firmly. "Go." She practically had to push him to get him started.

"Go on. You already have a lifetime of regrets. You don't need to add to the list," Clarice told him.

"Well....." Horace said softly. "Perhaps another time. I'm sure we'll see each other again sometime."

"There might not be another time. Or another chance..... Go! That's an order!" Harriet said, giving him 'that look' over her glasses to intimidate him, if nothing else.

Horace hesitantly and slowly walked to the plane. Phoebe saw him coming in their direction, gave Beatrix a quick goodbye and reminded her to come back next summer, then ran back to her mother and the others.

"Please, please, please, get in the plane, Grandfather," she said to herself, the first two fingers on both hands crossed.

"You don't think you'll have any trouble finding your way home, do you?" Horace asked.

She turned to look at him. "No. I will gain some altitude before I get over the lake, and a few miles out over the water I will be able to see Wisconsin. I will refuel near Milwaukee, fly west until I get to the Mississippi River, and then follow it up to Saint Paul. Unless there is a head wind I will be at Wold Chamberlain long before dark. If it is getting late, there is Lobb Field in Rochester. I won't need a navigator. Remember, I prefer to fly solo."

"I think we both do," he said.

"Tell you what, if you get bored here, I can introduce you to a nice little bunch of ruffians in the Twin Cities."

"Forget the ruffians, but I might just take you up on that if Phoebe doesn't learn how to play the piano better," he half-laughed.

We stayed by the plane as Beatrix tucked her hair into her leather helmet, then climbed into her cockpit. It was only when she shouted down to Fred, "Contact!" that he walked back to join his family.

The Stearman started on the second attempt, and once the engine was warmed up, Beatrix taxied slowly to the far end of the field. They could hear the engine powering up, and watched as it came racing down the field, lifting off easily. Beatrix gained altitude and circled, diving closer to the ground, then pulling up again before flying due west.

Theo put his hand on Horace's shoulder as they stood, waiting until the sound of the plane died away. "For a minute or two I thought you might be addicted to flying in those contraptions. I was beginning to worry we might be losing you. Glad you didn't go."

Horace chuckled slightly. "Beatrix flies solo." He paused, then added, "So do I."

Theo was about to say something, but thought better of it.

Phoebe was standing with her mother and Clarice, watching until the plane was out of sight. "Think you'll see her again?" Clarice asked.

"With Beatrix, who knows?" Harriet answered.

A smile came to Phoebe's lips. She whispered to herself, "She'll be back. I know she will."

ACKNOWLEDGMENTS
AND A FEW RANDOM THOUGHTS

In the summer of 2016, I self-published *The Great Saugatuck Murder Mystery*, and I was surprised and gratified that it was so well received. It wasn't long before people asked if there was going to be a sequel. I knew this mystery also had to be set in Saugatuck, preferably in the 1920s, and with the same characters. This time I added a few new ones.

I am deeply indebted to a small battalion of people who helped make this beach-book mystery a reality, starting with my wife Pat Dewey who was perpetually encouraging. She is the model on the front cover, taken from a painting done by her late husband Stan Wilson. Two great long-time friends, John Thomas and Peter Schakel, wore down pencils and went through ballpoint pens doing the editing work. And then, there is Sally Winthers who magically converted the manuscript into a book. Plus, all of my friends who kept up a steady stream of encouragement. With all of them, none of this would happened. Or, if you don't like the book – blame them.

I should probably trot out the legal disclaimer part. This is a work of fiction. Period. There never was a murder on the Meadow at Ox-Bow, or anywhere else out on the campus. Some of the characters are real – the folks from here in Saugatuck, notably my good friends Thomas and Bill from the Sand Bar, and Henry Gleason. The trio of musicians were also very real. Trix and Ollie were my uncles; Lloyd Stoddard was one of the finest Dixieland and jazz pianists anywhere in the Mid-west. I consider myself fortunate, in my all too short attempt at becoming a jazz bagpipe player, to play with him when he was with the Turkey River All Stars.

As for the rest of the characters – the Balfours, the Garwoods, Fred, Harriet and Phoebe, Beatrix the Intrepid Aviatrix, the police chief, the local physician, and Roletta Hansen the piano teacher, and a few others – all fiction.

There is no place in the world like Saugatuck. Waking up in the morning and eagerly anticipating what is about to unfold is one of the greatest of all possible joys. It's the beauty of this area, the support of the performing and visual arts, the restaurants and shops, but above all, it's the people. Truly, a day away from Saugatuck is a day wasted!

Made in the USA
Monee, IL
24 July 2020